The Treasured Heart

The Treasured Heart

WANDA TERRY

XULON PRESS

Xulon Press
2301 Lucien Way #415
Maitland, FL 32751
407.339.4217
www.xulonpress.com

© 2018 by Wanda Terry

All rights reserved solely by the author. The author guarantees all contents are original and do not infringe upon the legal rights of any other person or work. No part of this book may be reproduced in any form without the permission of the author. The views expressed in this book are not necessarily those of the publisher.

Unless otherwise indicated, Scripture quotations taken from the Holy Bible, New International Version (NIV). Copyright © 1973, 1978, 1984, 2011 by Biblica, Inc.™. Used by permission. All rights reserved.

Printed in the United States of America.

ISBN-13: 978-1-54564-673-1

Acknowledgements

I would like to thank both my sisters Leila Kerschensteiner and Peggy Orcutt for helping with editing and encouraging me on this book, Janelle Steer for helping on editing and my children Justin, Becky and Josh for loving me. Thank you as well, to my husband Tim for the cover art, your support and love. Most of all I thank God for giving me a story that still amazes me every day.

INTRODUCTION

It was a beautiful warm morning as I waited for my sister Leila to drive up in her shiny new black Grand Am Pontiac. I was delighted she was going to the court house with me, which is in Boise, the Capitol of Idaho. My stomach was tied in knots with anxiety thinking of the possibility of seeing my ex-husband, because of a child support hearing. My mind quickly wondered off to my younger days, before I gave birth to my two children, days of fun, no responsibilities, and when God was first and foremost in my life. I began remembering the feeling of when I was about six years old and I came home from church and felt the love of God so strong, I wanted to give him a present. The thought came to me like a light bulb going off in my head of what I was going to give Him. I went and found my younger sister Leila who was eighteen months younger than I and told her of my plan. We went and took a large spoon out of the silverware drawer and dug a hole large enough to bury one of our favorite toys. I reflect on it now and wonder why she gave up one of her favorite toys along with me. I was so excited I had done something amazing for God. It was so special to me; I had to go tell my oldest sister Peggy what we had accomplished. She smiled and giggled and told us, that's not how you give to God. She explained. "You put money in an offering plate at church." I was extremely disappointed with her explanation so we went and dug up our toys and tried to forget the big plan I had for God. It seemed though later in my life, God didn't forget the big plan He had for me at the courthouse. The story at the courthouse was not about my child support hearing, but of a meeting with a young fourteen year old girl, who knew absolutely nothing about God. Ana and I had a true encounter with God's power and love on that hot summer's day in July. I will never forget the joy I experienced as long as I'm alive on this side of heaven. From that point on at the court house, I created a fictional story of Ana's life, from my perspective. It was created with the help of God and his inspiration. I then put this amazing story into a book. The Treasured Heart.

CHAPTER 1

I'm sitting here on this hard bench which reminds me of a wooden pew that would be in an old country church. Really, I'm sitting on a bench in a hallway of the Ada County Courthouse, in Boise Idaho with my sister Leila. She has been most helpful and supportive of me since my divorce. I'm here trying to get child support from my ex-husband and it seems I'm always in a battle with him. Leila and I have already found out that we have missed the hearing we came for, and my attorney has gone to lunch. As it turns out, the hearing was earlier than we expected, so we have decided to wait for him.

While we wait, I can't help noticing a man and a young girl, sitting just four feet from us. The girl seems to be about the age of my fourteen-year-old son, Josh. I overhear the two of them talking. The halls are quiet, with only the occasional sound of a woman's high heels clicking on the marble floor. The man, who I assume is the girl's father, is not too bad looking, but seems to be worked up about something. As time goes on, his voice gets progressively louder. I hear him say the girl's mother is lying and how he can prove it. He thumbs through papers to show her proof of the lies her mother has told. A woman walks up to the man and the girl. She begins to speak sweetly to the girl, and I realize they must be mother and daughter. Suddenly, the man becomes boisterous and quite loud.

He yells at the mother, "Why are you pretending to be so nice?" A tall man was with the woman, who I think might be the girl's step-dad. He encourages the woman to leave, which she does but with obvious hesitation on her part. They see their attorney coming down the hall, briefly speak to him and he then ushers them into the large courtroom doors.

The dad tells the girl it's time to go into the courtroom, and then all hell breaks loose. The girl screams at her dad. "Why do you always do this to mom?"

"Do what?"

"You always have to yell at mom!" The girl begins crying. Her dad says they need to move along into the

Chapter 1

courtroom. As the man takes hold of her arm, she pulls away. He abruptly tells her to sit on the bench and he will see her later. She moves over to the bench where I'm sitting and sits down beside me.

That's when my conversation begins with her. With concern, I ask her if she's okay and she answers, "no." I listen as she talks to me and I ask her what her name is. She tells me her name is Ana. She's a cute girl, with sharp facial features and beautiful blue eyes. Her hair is dark blond and cut in a medium bob. She says she's tired of her parents fighting over her all the time.

"How old are you?" I ask.

Ana replies, "fourteen."

I tell her about my two sons, Josh who is the same age as she, and Justin who is 15. My sons stay with me most of the time, and rarely see their dad. Ana informs me that she lives with her dad and step-mom in Portland, Oregon and she often helps take care of her step-sisters.

Ana surprises me by asking, "Can I come and live with you?"

"I don't really get along with my ex- husband either," I tell her ignoring her question.

"My dad doesn't usually act like this. It's only when he gets around my mom and step-dad," Ana says.

Just then I see my attorney coming down the hall, so I stand up and walk toward him, with Leila right behind me. He tells us what had happened earlier that morning when we missed the court hearing. He apologizes for the misunderstanding of the change of the hearing time and explains what occurred at the hearing. The judge gave my ex-husband a chance to pay a small part of what he owes me for child support or face serving time in jail. I thank him, and we begin to leave, when a familiar voice, or as some call it, a still small voice, or a nudge from God, comes to me. I look over at Ana and God tells me to go talk to her. I tell God I already talked to her and at that I have no idea what I am going to say. I walk over to her and it's as if God takes over and helps me with the words that Ana so desperately needs to hear.

"Ana," I quietly say, as I look into her moist blue eyes, "do you know anything about God?"

"No." She softly replies

"Have you ever heard anything about angels?"

"Yes," she says.

Chapter 1

"Ana," I tell her, "I believe God put me here at this time and this place just to tell you that Jesus died on a cross for your sins. Would you like to accept Him as your personal Savior?"

Ana's response surprises me. "Yes," she answers.

"Okay, Ana. I'm going to pray with you. Just repeat these words after me."

"I want Jesus to come into my life. Amen."

"You know Ana, if God can send me to you, He can send others as well," I tell her. "Be on the lookout for those people He sends your way."

I give Ana a hug and leave the Courthouse.

Chapter 2

Wow, I feel as if my life is going to be different, Ana thought as she watched the two ladies walk up the stairs and out of her life. Let's see, what did the lady say her name was? Oh yeah, it was Wanda. Was this real or was she an angel? My parents never went to church or even talked much about God. I once went to church with my friend Angie, but my dad didn't want me to go after that. He said it was a bunch of fabricated religious stuff. "Jesus." Wanda said the name Jesus, but I don't really know much about Him except the baby Jesus at Christmas time. My grandma Kathy always had a manger scene of Mary, Joseph and baby Jesus sitting on her end table. That's all I really know about this Jesus. Why did I say yes to Wanda about accepting Jesus? She said, "Do you want to accept Jesus into your life?" I guess Wanda just seemed like such a nice person and I felt that I could trust her. All at once, a strange feeling came over me; it was as if I knew everything was going to be okay. A calm peaceful feeling filled me; like I had never felt before.

I usually hate to wait, but the time seemed to fly by while I was waiting for my parents to come back. Before I knew it, the door of the courtroom flew open and my Dad stormed out, walking right past me without talking to me at all. He just left! I couldn't believe it. After a few minutes my Mom came out with her attorney and my step-dad. She had tears in her eyes, but they weren't sad tears. She had a big smile shining on her face.

Mom came and stood directly in front of me and said, "Ana, you're going home with us."

After the events of the day I didn't know what to say or feel. My dad said such terrible things about my mom over the last year that I thought my dad would win the court case. My mom stood there looking at me, anxiously awaiting my reply. I knew I would miss my step-sisters and would feel lonely since I was mom's only child, but all I could say was, "What school do I go to?"

Mom laughed and pulled me close to her and hugged me like she would never let me go. It felt good. Really good!

CHAPTER 3

My mom and step-dad lived on the east side of Boise in a big house. They've decorated my bedroom in bright colors; purple, pink and green, unlike anything mom would ever choose. Mom said her friend Janice had helped her design the room. It was a nice change from the room dad had for me. That room was done in blues and beiges, which happen to be my dad's favorite colors, but not mine. I shared a bed with my sister. She's always stealing the covers from me and my dresser was way too small. At my mom's house, I sleep on a big double bed and have a nice big dresser of my own. My room has a window that overlooks a nice neighborhood park. It will be fun watching the neighborhood kids play in the park across the street. The park has three big swings, a couple of smaller swings and all sorts of slides. It also has a sandbox. It's not a very big sandbox, but the kids seem to enjoy it.

I will be starting my new school on Monday. I hope my dad sends my clothes to me. He seemed really upset when he left the court house. This school in Boise is different from the one I used to go to; since Mom and Jim bought a new house together across town, this one is a rival school. I had two friends at school I hadn't seen for several years. We did everything together. Their names were Sara and Riley. I called Riley when I first got home, and her mom told me she had gone to live with her dad in Seattle, Washington. She told me that Riley had a difficult time when I left to live with my dad and she had become a different person. Our friend, Sara, met a boy and was spending all her time with him, which left Riley without any friends. Riley's mom said she had become a recluse, staying in her room all the time. Riley then started dressing differently. Her mom told me Riley had met a new girl at school who had recently moved to Boise so they both hung out together. The new girls' name was Kim. She introduced pot to Riley, which then led to other drugs. Riley's mother told me how hard it was for her during

Chapter 3

that time and she was sad she had to send Riley to her dads to get her away from Kim. I could hear Riley's mom softly crying over the phone. I felt bad that I had brought up old memories, so I told her I was sorry about all that had happened and told her goodbye. My heart ached for Riley. We had been such good friends. It seems like divorce changes everything.

I then called Sara, but she wasn't home. Her mom said she was over at her boyfriend's house a lot. I told her I would call back later and said goodbye.

I thought to myself, "I'm really batting a thousand." The next few days passed quickly. Mom and I had to go shopping for new clothes for school which didn't hurt my feeling one bit. All I had was what I was wearing when I came to Boise.

Chapter 4

The first day of school was here and I was quite nervous. I didn't know anyone at this school. It was a large two story gray building. I hope I meet some nice kids. Mom and I left early so I could get there before school started and have time to get my new schedule. I found the office and went inside.

As I entered, I saw the secretary sitting at her desk. She was a middle-aged woman, nicely dressed. She appeared to be busy on the phone. As I went inside the door she looked up, her glasses hanging on the tip of her nose. She pushed them up and gave me a wave of her hand to let me know she saw me. I waited for a few minutes while she finished up on the phone. As she completed her phone call, she asked if she could help me. I told her who I was and that I needed to get my schedule.

"What's your name?"

Chapter 4

I told her my name again. I waited as she thumbed through some papers on her desk and pulled out what looked like my schedule. She handed it to me and asked a girl who had been sitting at a smaller desk across the room to take me around to see my classes. The secretary introduced me to her. Pam was a small girl, who seemed kind of shy. She had long, straight, dark brown hair, which was unbelievably shiny.

"Hi," Pam said. "Let's go." Pam showed me where all my classes were, in the order in which I had them. The school seemed so big; it had stairs that were generously wide, and we went from one end of the school to the other. We ended up in front of my locker, which was not close to any of my classes. Pam seemed a little quiet, as if she might not have many friends, but then again it seemed that wherever we went there was someone who greeted her.

Just as we got back to the office, the first bell rang to let everyone know that it was time to come into the school. Pam grabbed her books from the desk where she had been sitting, turns to me and then says, "I hope everything goes okay. Maybe I'll see you later." She turned and moved down the hall in the opposite direction and disappeared in the mass of kids in the hall.

Okay, now I was on my own. The halls filled up fast; they buzzed with talking and laughter. Maybe that would be me someday, I thought. I found my class and walked in; it felt as if everyone was looking at me. I guess it was only natural since I was the new girl at school. The teacher's name was Mr. Hansen. He's middle aged, at least to me that's what he seemed. Maybe it was the gray hair that made me think he was that old, after all he had a full head of hair. He directed me to the same page in the book that we were on in Portland. Thank God it was the same book and they weren't way ahead. I hate trying to catch up. The morning had flown by, and it was now time for lunch. "Oh, great, I don't know where the lunch room is," Ana realized.

Just then, a familiar voice said, "Oh, there you are."

It was Pam. I was so happy to see her!

"I was worried about you having lunch by yourself," Pam said as she took me to the cafeteria. We were greeted with a long line of students waiting to get their food. The aroma of Pizza was more than I could

Chapter 4

handle on an empty stomach. It smelled so good. After we got our food, she guided me to a table where four girls and two boys were already seated.

She introduced them to me and asked if it was all right if I sit with them. They said it was okay and I sat down next to one of the boys. There was Jan, Chelsea, Mandy, Kyla, Brandon, and Travis. They seemed very nice and I was grateful that I wouldn't be alone during lunch. While we ate our lunch, the room was abuzz with talking.

After we finished our lunch, we went outside. Time went by fast. We had only forty-five minutes for lunch break. I hoped that these kids would continue letting me hang out with them. They seemed different from my old friends. They didn't gossip about other kids, and they made me feel so welcomed. My other friends would never let someone new come into our group as Pam did. It made me feel good inside. At this point, I'll take whatever friends I can get.

The rest of the day seemed to drag more and more as the day went on. After the last class, I found my bus and went home. Mom surprised me and came home early to see how I did at school. My Mom is pretty;

she has blonde hair and blue eyes, like me. Her hair hangs down to her shoulders, with soft loose curls that bounce as she moves.

"How was your day, Ana?"

I described the day to her and she seemed pleased that everything had gone so well.

"Do you have much homework today?

I told her, "Just a little bit."

"Well, you'd better go upstairs and get it finished before dinner," she said as she drew me close to her and hugged me firmly. Then, whispering softly in my ear, she said, "I'm so glad you're here with us, Ana. I really missed you."

I finished my homework, which wasn't hard at all, went over to my bay window and sat on the bench that fit just inside the window. I began thinking about my day and how great it had gone, better than I thought it would. Then my thoughts returned to the courthouse and to Wanda who had told me that God would send other people along my path in life. Wow! I bet Pam was one of those people! I glanced out my window and down below at the park where a little girl was sitting in the sand box. I suddenly realized that something

Chapter 4

seemed strange about the little girl. She was just sitting there, doing nothing at all. As I watched her I noticed her hair had shimmers of red. She looked as if she was about five years old. I began wondering what she must be thinking about. She didn't move as she stared blankly into space. It seemed I had seen her before, sitting in that same spot.

Just then Mom called me down for dinner. Mom was a very good cook. My step-dad, Jim, came home and we all sat down to eat my favorite meal, spaghetti. She made the best spaghetti I'd ever eaten. I had been looking forward to it ever since I arrived here. Jim is a nice enough man, but he doesn't talk much. I really don't know him that well either. He's kind of a big man and can be intimidating if you don't know him. I hadn't really talked to him much, so I thought maybe I would ask him about his family. He was married before he met Mom; I think they worked together for the State of Idaho.

I asked Jim if he had any kids. Jim answered me with his fork in mid-air and spaghetti dangling. "I have two; a boy who is 28. His name is Brent and a girl 24; her name is Tish. Brent is married and has two kids;

Breanne who is two years old and James who is four years old." Jim nonchalantly sat his fork back on his plate and continued. "James is named after me. Tish isn't married yet, although she just finished college and is engaged to be married next year. They all live in Denver, Colorado. Sometimes I wish I lived closer to them." Jim seemed to open up to me, explaining how much he missed his kids and Denver at times. He explained that he lived in Denver when his kids were small. After his divorce, he moved closer to his parents. He told me they were both having health problems and since he was an only child, he needed to move closer to them. "They are both deceased now, but I have you and your mom to keep me company and Boise is home to me now."

Out of the blue Jim exclaimed, "Maybe we can all go to Denver for Christmas this year! That would be so much fun! Don't you think so, Karen?" I'd never heard Jim talk so much! Jim finally finished his fork full of spaghetti which he had almost forgotten.

"Mom, that sounds like a lot of fun. Can we go?"

Mom reminded me that I might be with my dad for Christmas this year, and she wasn't sure yet. I felt

Chapter 4

a little disappointed because it would be nice to get to know Jim's kids. Maybe I could get a little insight into this quiet man mom is married to, or maybe he's not so quiet after all.

Chapter 5

It seemed odd that Dad hadn't tried to contact me since I moved to Boise. We were so close, or at least I thought we were. I hope the girls are okay. I think about them often. Maybe I'll try to call Dad a little later tonight. "Mom is it okay if I call Dad tonight?"

"Sure honey, but don't wait too long. You'll need to go to bed soon."

I watched a little TV with Jim and Mom, told them goodnight, then went upstairs and called Dad. I had butterflies in my stomach as I dialed Dad's number. The phone rang several times and then my six-year old stepsister Katie answered.

"Hello."

"Hi Katie, this is Ana."

"Ana, we miss you so much! When are you coming home?"

Chapter 5

"It might be awhile before I can see you all." I told her I missed her too. She is a cute little girl who has a sweet personality and the cutest little button nose.

I asked her what she'd been up to since I've been gone, and she answered, "I lost my two front teeth. You should see how funny I look."

"I bet you look adorable."

She giggled, and I could tell someone grabbed the phone from Katie's hand and yelled into my ear. "What do you want?" snapped my stepmother Debbie.

I was so shocked and surprised by what I had just heard that it took a minute to figure out what to say. Tentatively, I finally said, "I just want to talk to my dad."

She snapped again, "Your dad took Amy, (my other little stepsister), to her soccer practice."

I managed to get out of my mouth, a fast, "Thank you, I'll try back later" and quickly hung up. I stood there with my mouth hanging open in disbelief. Why is she so mad at me? I don't remember being rude or mean to her. I always tried to be nice to her; Dad would have a fit if I didn't behave around Debbie. I always helped take care of the girls. Maybe that's it. Yeah, I'm sure that has to be it, I thought to myself.

I decided I might as well go to bed to be rested for school the next day. I woke the next morning with the sun shining in my window. I lay there thinking about the day ahead, wondering if I would get to be with Pam and her friends again. Since I was taking the bus today I decide to head out a little early to make sure I don't miss it. As I left the house, Mom explained to me where I needed to go to catch the bus.

Let's see, what was the bus number, I thought to myself. Oh yeah, 343. I think that's what mom told me. As I walked closer to the place where mom told me to go, I noticed about eight kids were already there. One is a familiar face, its Travis, Pam's friend.

As I walked closer, he saw me and put his hand up waving to me.

"Hi Ana, it's good to see you."

"Hi, Travis, it's good to see you too."

"You must live close to me," said Travis. "Where do you live?"

"I live over on that street over there," as I pointed to the street where I live. Travis then showed me, by pointing to the street where he lived, and it was the

Chapter 5

street right behind mine. That would be funny if we lived right behind each other.

"My house is the green one with the beige trim," he said.

"Mine is the beige house with the maroon trim." We both realized that indeed, we lived directly behind each other. Both of us busted up laughing.

"That's great! Maybe we can walk to the bus together," Travis suggested, "if you don't mind."

"That sounds good to me."

"I don't hang out with the other kids at the bus stop much," he whispered to me.

I asked, "Why not?"

"They think I'm different because I'm a Christian." He waited for my reaction and then asked, "Do you go to church?"

"No." I could see his expression sink as I said it, and then I quickly added. "But I'm a believer."

His smile returned to his face and then he asked, "How come you don't go to church?"

I began to tell him my story about Wanda and the courthouse. Just then, the bus came. Once we were on the bus, I continued telling him my story. Travis was so easy to talk to and attentive as he listened.

"You should come to my church," Travis told me as we neared the school. "Pam and my other friends all go there as well."

"Do all the kids I met yesterday go there?"

"Yes. I want you to meet our Pastor. He's amazing! His name is Dave. We have Bible studies and do all kinds of fun things as well, like miniature golf, bowling, swimming, snow tubing and a lot of other things."

"It all sounds great, but I have never gone to church and I really don't know anything about the Bible."

"That's okay," said Travis, "that's how you learn; I don't know everything about the Bible either. It'll be fun!"

At lunch, my new friends were encouraging me to visit their church. "I'll have to ask my mom first," I told them. My new friends are so great! They seem to look after me by making sure I'm not alone and I like that a lot about them.

That night, I asked my mom about going to church with my new friends.

"What kind of church is it?" Mom asked.

Chapter 5

I didn't even think about asking them what kind of church it was. I didn't think it would be a problem. Mom advised me I should find out first. I told her I would. I went upstairs to do my homework and in the corner of my eye I saw the same little girl sitting in the same spot she was yesterday as I passed by my window. I thought it was so strange how she just sat there with that same blank stare. I again wondered what she must be thinking.

I finished my homework and went downstairs for dinner.

"How's school going, Ana?" Jim asked.

"It's going great, so far." Jim seemed delighted. "I've made some new friends."

"Maybe they can all come over for pizza, so we can meet them, sometime."

It made me feel good that Jim would be interested in my friends. He told me he enjoyed having a nice young lady such as me in their home. He made me feel great. Maybe he was just trying to be nice. No, I need to be grateful to him and have a more positive attitude; yes, that's what I'm going to do. Dad seemed to always say bad things about Jim. I guess maybe

Dad's a bit jealous or something. That reminds me; I needed to try calling Dad again. I ran upstairs and dialed Dad's number. As it rang, I prayed that my stepmother Debbie wouldn't answer. It rang; once, twice, and on the third ring I heard someone pick up the phone. Thankfully, it was Dad. Wow, God answered my prayer.

"Hello."

"Hi Dad!"

I held my breath as he spoke to me. "Oh, Ana, I'm so glad you called back. I heard you wanted to talk to me. How are you?"

"I'm doing great! I made some new friends." He didn't seem as excited as I had hoped he would be.

"Are mom and Jim treating you alright?"

"Yes."

"Be sure and call me if they don't treat you right."

"I will, dad."

"Well, I have to go now. I'll call you soon."

It was nice to talk to Dad, but it would be nice if he wouldn't be so jealous of Mom and Jim all the time. Maybe there was something about the whole situation that I didn't understand.

Chapter 5

Later that night I simply prayed. "God, please help my dad." That's all I could think of. "My dad needs help, but I don't know how to help him, but I think you do. Amen."

The next morning, I was so surprised to see Travis at my front door. He came to walk with me to the bus stop. I told him about what my dad had said and how I had prayed for him. He told me he was proud of me for turning to God for help. He told me God was the one who could change people's hearts.

I was really enjoying my time at school. The days raced by quickly. Mom had said it was okay for me to go to church with Travis, so I began going to church with Travis and my new friends. It turned out that the church was a non-denominational church named The Living Word. Travis was right about Pastor Dave. He was just as awesome as Travis had said he was.

The weekends went great as well. Every night I looked out my window to see if the same little girl was there sitting at the sand box and as sure as there is a sun, she was always there. It was starting to turn a little cooler as it was beginning to go into Idaho's Indian summer. During the day, it was warm, but toward evening it grew colder and colder. I thought maybe the next day I would go down to the park. I would like to go tonight, but I have a lot of homework to do. I must study for a big test tomorrow in U.S. Government. The next day, I looked out the window to see if the little girl was at the park, and to my surprise she wasn't there. Wouldn't you know, as soon as I decide to go talk to her, she doesn't show up? I should have gone yesterday. I checked every day from that day on and she wasn't there. A gloomy feeling came over me. Was it something about the little girl at the park? The feeling continued to get worse and worse. I tried to put away these dark feelings of gloom, wishing I could put them in a drawer and close it tight for good. But as fast as I shut it, the drawer keeps flying back open. I pray that God will take these feelings of gloom from me.

CHAPTER 6

Later that night, Mom came into my room and said, "Ana, I have something I need to talk to you about." Mom sat on the bed and patted the spot beside her. "Come sit here beside me."

I sat on the bed and looked up at her. She had a tear running down her cheek. I knew then that it was going to be bad. What could it be? Did Dad die, or something happen to one of the girls? The only time I had ever seen Mom cry was the time when she had found out Dad was cheating on her. She was a very strong woman, so I knew what she was about to tell me wasn't going to be good. I couldn't stand it any longer, so I asked her, "Mom, what's the matter?"

"I've been to the doctor and he found a lump in my breast."

I sat there frozen, like a piece of ice.

"I'm going to have surgery. The doctor thinks they can get all the cancer."

"Cancer, you have cancer?" I yelled. I just couldn't help it, I was so upset.

"Ana, it will all be fine. The doctor thinks the surgery will take care of it and everything will return to normal." Mom took me into her arms and held me close. I felt comforted as she held me. Now I knew why I had that feeling of gloom. The next day, I asked all of my friends to pray for my mom.

The surgery went great and the doctor seemed to think he had gotten it all and there was no cancer in the lymph nodes. Pastor Dave came to see Mom at the hospital. I was a little worried about how Mom would react to having him come see her.

He introduced himself, "Hello! I'm Pastor Dave. Your daughter Ana has been coming to our church. She's been a great asset to our youth group." He told my mom that I had suggested some different ideas for the group and had lit a flame within their hearts. "Most of the kids have gone to church all of their lives, but I understand this is Ana's first experience with a church," he added.

Chapter 6

As Dave was talking, I walked into the room.

"Oh, hi, Ana," he said. He walked over and gave me a big hug. Then, turning to my mom, he asked, "Would it be all right if I pray with you?"

"I would love that."

He said a short prayer, knowing Mom wasn't accustomed to being prayed for. I was surprised she agreed to let him pray with her at all. Dave squeezed her hand and told her if there was anything he could do, to let him know, and then he left.

Jim walked in just about then, walked over to Mom, and gave her a short kiss. "Who was that?"

"That was Ana's pastor, Dave. He seems like such a nice man."

"Oh yes, he's great!" I announced.

We stayed with Mom until she went to sleep. Jim drove us home, and on the way, he seemed kind of quiet. I asked him if he was doing okay and he broke down and said, "I just don't think I can live without your Mom, Ana." A tear fell down his cheek. I didn't know what to say. I hadn't ever seen Jim like this before. I reassured him that she would be okay. Then, to my amazement, I was saying, "God will never leave us nor forsake us. That's a promise."

"I hope God doesn't start now," he added.

I answered back with confidence, "He won't." When we reached home, I went up to my room and sat by my window and thought of Mom. The park across the street was all lit up from the street light. That's when I saw her. The little girl was sitting in the sandbox. What was she doing out this late at night? Just then she looked up at me and smiled. I smiled back, grabbed my coat and ran outside. By the time I got to the sandbox, she was gone. Why did her parents allow her to be out here by herself? I just don't understand. Sadly, I went back into the house and got ready for bed. As I said my prayers, I asked God to take special care of Mom and help her body to heal quickly. Then I added, "Lord, please keep that little girl in your tender care, in Christ's name, Amen."

Chapter 7

According to the doctors, Mom's recovery from her surgery was exceptional. Her body healed faster than anyone had expected, and I know without a doubt it was God's hand that helped Mom to get better so quickly.

Thanksgiving was soon approaching, and we were going over to my mom's sister's house for Thanksgiving. Aunt Peggy lives in Mountain Home, a small town about 45 minutes from Boise. She has a husband Dick, and two boys, Don and Tracy. They are a little older than I am. My aunt is a great cook. We always have a ton of food to eat and the best part is Aunt Peggy's apple pie. My grandma and grandpa are there also, and Grandpa loves my aunt's pie. He takes a huge piece with lots of whipping cream. I think Aunt Peggy made it just for him, because he loves it so much. Mom and I help Aunt Peggy clean up after we are all finished eating the delicious meal.

After we're finished with the cleanup, it's time for a rousing game of Jenga. It's a game with sticks that are stacked about ten inches tall. You pull a piece of wood out without the stack of wood falling and then put it back on top of the stack. If you make them fall, you lose. Grandpa had very shaky hands and every time it was his turn we all thought he would make them fall. But to our amazement, that didn't happen. He always made it through his turn without making the stack fall. When it was my turn, and after several minutes of deliberation on which piece of wood to pull out, I made my choice, even though there weren't many choices left. I pulled on it slowly, and then it happened; they all fell with a loud crash onto the table. We all had a good laugh. Grandpa was proud of himself for outlasting all of us. We played over, and over again, and he never lost one of the games.

The days before Christmas zoomed by fast. Mom helped me buy presents for my step-sisters and she even helped me buy presents for my step-mom and dad. Jim and I spent a Saturday together buying

Chapter 7

Mom's present. The mall was ringing with the sounds of Christmas and was filled with wall to wall people. Jim bought Mom her favorite perfume and a ring; she had shown it to him earlier, so he couldn't go wrong. Jim helped me pick out a sweater; it was pink and white and very soft. Mom went with me to buy something for Jim. Mom said that Jim loves tools and likes to build things in the garage. I bought a tool for him, even though I don't know how the tool is used, I'm sure he will know exactly how it's used.

Christmas vacation began three days before Christmas and the day after our vacation began, I was leaving for Portland to spend Christmas with my dad and his family. Travis surprised me by stopping by and giving me a present before I left.

"Please don't open it until Christmas," Travis said.

"Okay" I replied. "Oh wait; I have something for you too." I ran to my room upstairs to get a small box from my dresser. As I crossed the room, I noticed the little girl was sitting in the sand box again. What's up with this girl? It's so cold outside. The girl had to be freezing. But Travis was waiting for me downstairs, so I grabbed his Christmas present and ran down the stairs. I was halfway down and stopped. I could hear Mom and Travis talking to each other. I paused a moment to see if I could tell what they were saying, but just then they saw me, so I continued down the stairs. I scurried past them and opened the door, looking out to see if the little girl was still at the sand box. As I feared, she was gone.

"What are you doing, Ana?" Mom asked.

I explained about how I kept seeing a little girl sitting in the sand box in the park. They both agreed that it was a little strange. I gave Travis his present and asked him to please not open it until Christmas. After Travis left, I asked Mom what they were talking about.

"Oh honey, he was telling me what he got you for Christmas." Mom replied.

"What did he get me?" I asked.

"You never were good at waiting for Christmas to open your presents." Mom giggled and put her arm around my neck. "Come in here Ana. Jim and I have something for you."

We went into the living room and gathered around the Christmas tree. Mom always went all out when decorating the Christmas tree. She wanted it to be

Chapter 7

special for us every year. This year it seemed to be extra special. It was always a thing of beauty. She had decorated it with gold balls and had woven red ribbons throughout the tree. It also had thousands of lights. There, underneath the tree, was a box wrapped beautifully in gold paper and a red bow. Mom handed me the box and told me to unwrap it. Mom had used tons of tape to keep me from looking inside. I finally tore off the wrapping and there was a plain brown box. Inside was a maroon colored Bible. I had wanted one for some time. It was just the kind I wanted, a New International Version Study Bible. It even had my name inscribed on it. How had they known what kind I wanted? I bet Travis helped them pick it out.

I hugged them both and thanked them. "I love it!" Then they handed me another present. It was a card. Inside was a sheet of paper with writing. It said, "Ana, this is to let you know that when you get back from your Dad's house, you get to start taking skiing lessons. You also have everything you need for skiing in the garage. We thought it would be nice for you to ski with all your friends, since they all ski and you were the only one in your group that didn't. You are such a great daughter, you deserve the best. We love you, Mom and Jim."

I was so excited that I bolted out the door and into the garage! Just inside the door there were skis, poles, boots, and clothes! Wow, this was great! I could hardly wait to go skiing.

"Mom can you guys open your presents too?" I handed them both their presents. Mom seemed to really like her sweater. She held it up against her, showing us how it would look when she wore it. I could tell it would look great on her. Then Jim opened his package. He seemed to light up with delight as he saw the tool I had bought for him. He told me it would come in handy.

I had been hoping to go to the Christmas Eve service at church, but I had to leave to go to Portland to see Dad. Oh well, maybe next year we can all go.

Chapter 8

I was a little nervous about seeing Dad and Debbie. He was so angry the last time I saw him. I asked my friends to pray for me while I was gone. It gave me a lot of comfort to know they would be praying for me. Dad was waiting for me at the airport when I arrived, and it was so nice to see his smiling face when I went through the doors. He gave me a big hug and told me he was excited to see me. We picked up my luggage and went to the car. It had been raining, just as one expects in Portland. He drove the familiar freeway to the house I once lived in, where I found things hadn't changed much since I had left months before. Dad told me he was glad I came here for Christmas, but he needed to tell me something. I thought, oh great what's wrong now? He paused for a moment before continuing.

"Well, Debbie and I have this Christmas Eve thing we have to go to tonight. Her best friend Roni is having her big party again this year. As a matter of fact, Debbie's already there, so I'm hoping you'll watch the girls for us, like you did last year."

I was very relieved that I didn't have to deal with Debbie quite yet, so I answered back promptly, "Sure Dad, that's no problem at all." We pulled into the driveway and parked in the garage. My heart raced. I didn't know how the girls were going to react to my being here.

Just as we opened the doors of Dad's SUV, the door to the house opened. Katie ran to me, jumped into my arms, and hugged me tightly. She sobbed into my neck, hardly able to talk. Finally, she spoke, "Ana, Ana, I missed you so much!" Then I heard another voice; it was my other sister, Becka. She also hugged me tight and it made me feel as if I had never left. Becka is eight years old and a smart girl, with her head always in a book. I was surprised she took the time to come greet me.

"Ana, you're staying in my room," said Katie. She talked so fast I could hardly understand her. She told

Chapter 8

me she was glad I was home for Christmas. "We can spend lots of time together and have fun."

Becka helped carry my bags into Katie's room. We all sat down on Katie's bed and I asked how they had both been. Becka began telling me about Dad and how he was when he returned home after the court hearing. Becka said that he was so upset about how things had turned out that he had moped around the house for days, and nothing they did was good enough for him. "Poor Mom, got it the worst," said Becka. "One day mom must have had enough because she told him she was going to leave him if he didn't straighten up."

"He's been better since then," said Becka. "Dad really misses you Ana, and we do too."

I told the girls that I missed everyone too, but I liked living in Boise and I had made some great friends. Boise is a great city; it doesn't rain as much, and it's not as big as Portland. I even go to church and belong to the youth group there. Katie couldn't believe I went to church now. I told her about the lady at the courthouse and how I had accepted Jesus into my life.

"You did what?"

I explained to them about Jesus and how He died on the cross for our sins. They weren't quite sure about all I was telling them because they hadn't heard anything about Jesus before, as far as I knew.

"You mean you're like those kids at school who have Bible study at lunch and pray at the flag pole once a year?"

"Yes, that's who I am. Some kids call us Jesus freaks, but I don't care what they call me. I love Jesus!" I exclaimed.

"What's Dad going to say about this?" Becka asked.

"I'll tell him just what I told you; I'm not ashamed of my belief."

"Wow, you really have changed, haven't you Ana?" Becka asked as she turned and went out of the bedroom.

I stood there a moment and thought about what Becka had said and realized how much I had changed. It was Christmas Eve, and in a way, I wished that I was home in Boise with Mom and Jim. I missed Travis and all my other friends.

I spent the rest of Christmas Eve trying to make it a special night for the girls. I made popcorn and hot chocolate as a snack for all of us while we watched

Chapter 8

the movie, "A Christmas Story". The girls had never seen it before and they really liked it. After the movie, it was time to tuck the girls into bed, but before I did that, I helped them set cookies and milk out for Santa. We were all excited for Christmas day to come. I finally got the girls tucked in bed, and then I quietly got into bed, said a quiet prayer for a Merry Christmas celebration with my family, and drifted off to sleep.

Morning came early. I awoke to Katie's and Becka's grabbing at my feet and shaking me. I just about jumped out of my skin. They were giggling and begging me to get up. I looked at the clock and was surprised to see that it was four in the morning. I told them they should go back to bed. They both began to pull me out of bed onto the floor. I fell with a thud.

Katie looked at Becka and shouted, "Look what you've done now!"

Becka yelled back, "You did it too!"

I whispered, "You guys need to be quiet, you'll wake everyone up."

We all began laughing as I got up off the floor. I put on my robe and we tip toed down the stairs. We were almost at the bottom of the staircase when from out of nowhere someone jumped out of the dark and shouted "boo!" We all nearly ran into each other trying to run back up the stairs. Someone switched on the light and began laughing hysterically. It was Dad. I've never heard him laugh like that before. He motioned for us to come back down and told us he had never seen three girls so scared in all his life.

Dad tried to compose himself and asked, "Ok girls, what are you doing up so early?"

"The girls couldn't sleep so they decided to come and wake me up."

Dad said that Debbie was still sleeping, and we needed to go back to bed and try to get a little more sleep, at least until seven o'clock.

The girls, both at the same time whined, "Not till seven?"

Dad said "Yes, seven, and if you argue with me any more I'll make it eight o'clock."

They raced up the stairs and back into their room. Dad and I made our way back up to our beds. Thank goodness! I was so tired. Seven o'clock came too soon. It seemed as if I had been asleep for only a minute

Chapter 8

when the girls came running in as if they had slept all night.

"Ana, Ana, come on, let's go downstairs." Katie said, as I struggled to open my right eye and then the other.

I stretched my arms high into the air and sluggishly pulled myself out of bed. After putting on my robe, the girls grabbed my arms, one on each side and excitedly pulled me toward the door.

I pulled away from their grip and said, "Girls, I really have to go to the bathroom first." I turned down the hallway and went into the bathroom. The girls were right on my heels. I turned and told them, "You two need to wait out here."

This bathroom was the girl's bathroom. It's quite a large bathroom, so the girls share it. Debbie had done a good job at decorating the house; it's beautiful with dark rich wood and touches of cream and red. As I finished up in the bathroom, I thought to myself, this is Jesus' birthday. I softly murmured, "Happy Birthday, Jesus, I love you so much." Then I heard whispers outside the door.

"Ana, hurry up," Becka whispered softly.

I opened the door to two excited little girls. They could barely contain their excitement. We went down the stairs and there sitting on the love seat were Dad and Debbie in their robes. Dad got up, walked over to me and gave me a big hug, then went back and sat down next to Debbie.

Debbie uttered, "Good morning."

Dad told us that we should sit on the couch, so the girls and I did as we were told and sat on the couch. The Christmas tree lights were on and it looked stunning. It had hundreds of white lights that twinkled like the stars on a clear night. There were red and green balls all over the tree with red ribbons flowing around the tree. At the top was a white angel with a touch of red in her dress. She was the most gorgeous angel I had ever seen. There were presents everywhere. The girls could hardly wait to open theirs; they kept begging Dad to let them start opening them. But Dad just took his time, stalling, making them wait. I sat there wondering what there could possibly be under the tree for me. Dad stood up and began speaking.

"Ana, since you are kind of a special guest, we've all decided you should play Santa Claus this year."

Chapter 8

It was always a special deal to be Santa Claus, but somehow it didn't matter that much to me, like it used to. I smiled and handed out the packages, beginning with the girls. Soon, they had a big stack of presents in front of them. I placed my presents to one side. After all the presents had been handed out, we each opened our presents at the same time. My first present was a light blue sweater, then a necklace. I also opened a box of perfume. Then there was a huge box. What could this possibly be? I began opening it and to my amazement it was a computer. I had always wanted a computer, one that was my own.

Dad asked, "Do you like it, Ana?"

I was just about to tell Dad and Debbie thanks when Dad said, "That isn't all Ana. See that envelope on the top of the box? You need to open it as well." Inside the envelope was a card. On the inside of the card there was some writing. I began reading. It said, "Ana, this is for you to use for schoolwork. We are all hoping you will want to stay with us. The judge said you could be back with us after three months if you chose to. We all miss you so much! Please come home to us! We love you so much!" It was signed by them all; Dad, Debbie, Becka, and Katie. I couldn't believe what I had read. I hadn't expected anything like this to happen.

Dad waited a minute and then he asked. "What do you think, Ana? Do you want to come home and live with us?"

My stomach sank to the floor as Dad waited for my reply. A hundred thoughts raced through my head. I thought of Mom, how we've grown closer and how I've gotten to know Jim and enjoy his witty ways. Then there were my friends, especially Travis. I didn't want to give them all up. What was I going to do? Dad's going to be so mad if I don't stay with him. Time seemed to be frozen for an eternity while all these thoughts raced through my head.

But then Dad's voice rang in my ear. "What are you thinking, Ana?"

What was I going to say?

Dad repeated. "What are you going to do?"

So finally, out of my mouth came, "You know this was quite a surprise, and I think it would be best to think about it for a few days."

Chapter 8

He quickly barked. "Think about it, why do you need to think about it?"

"Dad don't get upset. I don't want to ruin the girls' Christmas," I pleaded.

"I'm sorry, honey; I just want you back so much. I was hoping that you would just say yes; please just say you'll stay," he begged. Dad was one who didn't give up easily.

"Come on Dad, you know I miss you all, but I need time to think it over." Hoping he would give it up for now, I finally told him I would let him know tomorrow at the latest. That seemed to satisfy him for now. Debbie piped in and tried to get the subject changed back to the girls and what they got for Christmas. I was so grateful to her for getting things back to a little more fun time for the girls. Katie got a doll and a lot of toys. Becka got some toys and some new ski equipment. She's been skiing since she was five years old. Debbie told me she's very good at it. Sometimes they take her up to Mt. Hood and they all go skiing except Katie; she hadn't wanted to learn yet. Dad and Debbie opened the presents I had brought and they seemed delighted with my choices.

The rest of the day went smoothly. We went to Debbie's sisters' house for Christmas dinner. I always enjoyed being around Linda. She has a good sense of humor. Her husband, Tim, did all the cooking, which was very good. They have two kids; Jason 4 and Meagan 6. They were cute little kids, with curly brown hair, and a lot of energy. Katie had fun playing with the two of them. I dreaded the day coming to an end because I knew the next day I had to tell Dad my decision. I tried not to think about it any more than I had to.

There were presents for everyone. I opened mine to the surprise of a new night gown. We had a nice time with Debbie's family and then after a long day we went home. I went up to my room, undressed and put on my new nightgown. It was soft and warm. I lay on my bed and stared at the ceiling. What am I going to do? I don't want to stay here. I don't want to hurt Dad, and I know he's going to be real mad if I choose to live with Mom. Just thinking about it makes me feel sick. Maybe I should stay here for awhile. I argued with myself, going back and forth. I put my hands up to my head and began banging it with my fists. "I can't

Chapter 8

stand this," I yelled at myself. I must have hit some sense into me, because all at once a light went off in my head. I hadn't opened the present Travis sent with me for Christmas. I retrieved it from my suitcase and opened it as if it was life or death, ripping it without hesitation. There inside the box shined the most stunning cross I had ever seen. I gently took it out of the box, draped it over my hand and looked at it intensely. While I looked at the cross I began thinking about Travis, and how much I missed him. I knew what I had to do. Travis was always telling me to give it to God and pray about it. He also would tell me that life is hard, but God is good, whenever I would have a problem. It was from a song he really liked. I decided I needed to get down on my knees and pray.

I began with, "Dear father God. I love you and I need your guidance. I don't know what to do. Please give me your wisdom to know how to handle this situation with my dad. Amen." I looked inside the box again and found a small piece of paper. I pulled it out and realized it was a note. I began reading: "Ana, I was praying for you the other night and God put the thought into my mind that you would feel troubled while you are away, so I wanted you to know that I'm praying for you until you get home." He signed it, "God loves you, and I love you," Travis. I then knew what I had to do, and it was going to be extremely difficult. I went to bed and that's when I felt a peace about what I had to do.

I woke up the next morning and went downstairs to breakfast. There sitting at the table alone, was Dad.

I asked, "Where is everybody?"

Dad replied, "They all went to exchange some gifts. You know how I am. I hate all those people running into me and waiting in line, so I decided to stay home with you."

I instantly felt ill. This was it, I'm going to have to tell Dad my decision and it wasn't going to be easy. "Lord, please help me," I prayed in silence.

Dad began to talk, "Ana, I just want you to know how much I love you. I don't want this to be hard on you, but I really want you to live with us."

I started to talk when he interrupted me. "Ana, let me finish, please. I decided you need to do what you think is best for you, so I'm prepared for whatever

Chapter 8

you decide will be the right choice for you." I couldn't believe my ears. He didn't seem mad at all.

I began speaking, "Well Dad, I have made a decision, although it was a difficult one. I'm glad you're not going to be mad at whatever I choose to do. I decided to go back and be with mom." I waited for him to say something and he just sat there, not saying anything.

Finally, with a tear sliding down his face, he looked right at me, smiled and said, "I wish you had made a different choice, but its okay." He leaned over and gave me a kiss on the cheek and then asked me what I wanted to do the rest of the day. I was in shock. I could hardly think of what to say.

Dad jumped in and asked if I wanted to go bowling. I had never gone bowling with Dad, but I had gone with my friends from church. I had shown some improvement since the first time I had gone with Travis. He was very good at it and I just kept throwing the ball into the gutter. Travis showed me I was holding the ball wrong and after that my game improved a little. I never got as good as Travis, but I could beat my friend Pam and my other girlfriends. I told Dad that bowling sounded like fun and it shouldn't be crowded unless everyone else in town had the same idea.

I was right. There weren't many people at the bowling alley at all. We rented our shoes and found bowling balls that fit our hands and then we found our lane. We began to bowl, and Dad was surprised to see that I could bowl as well as I did. The first game my score was 156 and Dad's was 182. I found out when Dad was young and before I was born he was on a bowling league and was very good. To my amazement I didn't throw any gutter balls. It also amazed me when all the pins would explode, and I would get a strike. We bowled again, and I almost beat Dad. He had 164 and I had 160.

"We should make a bet on the next game," he said.

"What kind of a bet?" I asked.

"Let's see, how about if you win I pay you fifty bucks, and if I win, you stay here in Portland with us," as he spoke with a straight face.

Oh great, I thought to myself. He doesn't give up easily.

Then, quickly, he laughed and said, "Just kidding." I never in my life was so glad to hear he was kidding.

Chapter 8

I gave him a big hug and then we decided to leave. We left and got a bite to eat at Dad's favorite restaurant, Elmers, where I think I had the best time I've ever had with my Dad. He seemed so at ease and relaxed. I thought maybe I would talk to him about my new life with my church friends, but somehow it didn't really feel like the right time for that, so I didn't. We finally went home, and Debbie and the girls were there. The girls were all excited about their treasures they had found earlier that day.

The week went by fast. We were busy every day. We played games with the girls and I went to the mall with some of my old friends. They told me they couldn't believe how much I'd changed. I told them about my new friends and how I go to church, but they didn't seem to want to hear about that kind of stuff. They changed the subject every time I mentioned anything about church.

Soon it was time for me to return home to Boise. I could hardly wait to see Mom, Jim, and all my friends. The girls kept begging me to stay, and I reassured them I would come to visit as soon as I could. Dad didn't say anything to me about staying, which was a big relief.

While I worked on packing my luggage for the trip home, Dad and Debbie packed up my new computer for me, so we could ship it to Boise on the airplane. Finally, it was time to leave. I said my goodbyes to the girls and Debbie. I was glad that Debbie and I seemed to get along a lot better than we ever had before. Dad drove me to the airport and he was quiet, until we were almost there. He began telling me he was happy I came to Portland for Christmas.

He said, "Ana, you made Christmas very special for all of us. I am very proud of what a wonderful young lady you've become."

It brought tears to my eyes as he spoke. "Dad, it's only because of my new faith in God. He's changed me inside and out."

Dad sat there quietly for a moment and said, "Maybe there is something to that religious stuff after all."

Tears swelled in my eyes and ran slowly down my cheek. I had never talked to Dad about my faith, but he must have seen it in me. I mumbled, "I love you, Dad."

"I love you too, Ana."

Dad dropped me off at the airport, we said our goodbyes, and then I went inside. While I was waiting

Chapter 8

to board the plane, my thoughts went over and over all that had happened in the last two weeks. I hoped they all enjoyed my stay as much as I did. It seemed as if they did. The girls had grown and seemed more independent. They both depended on me for everything when I lived with them. Now they both did things on their own, which made things easier for me.

As I boarded the plane, standing off to one side, was a little girl with an older lady. The little girl looked familiar to me. I couldn't help staring at her. Just as if a light bulb went off in my head, I realized who the little girl was. She was the girl in the sandbox at the park with long dark hair, across the street from where Mom lives. I wondered who the older woman was. Maybe it is her grandma or an aunt. I found my seat on the plane and noticed the little girl was sitting at the back of the plane. The flight was smooth, taking only an hour to get to Boise. It was good to see the lights of Boise on my side of the plane. I recognized certain buildings as we flew over the city. I hoped Mom and Jim were there at the airport. The plane landed without incident, taxied and pulled into the gate. I could hardly wait until I was able to exit the plane, but I was by the window and towards the middle, so there were a lot of people crowding the aisle to get out. I waited until it cleared. As I began to scoot my way to the aisle and stand up, I bumped into the little girl from the park. She said she was sorry and hurried past me with her grandma, or whoever she was, right behind her. I waited until it was clear enough to stand in the aisle and retrieved my carry-on. I walked out of the plane expecting to see Mom and Jim, when just then, I spotted a face I didn't expect to see. It was Travis standing at the back of the crowd of people swarming like bees greeting their loved ones. He spotted me and began to make his way over to me, then stood in front of me and said with a big smile, "Welcome back, Ana!"

"Thanks! It's great to be back, Travis."

He reached for my bag and I told him, "I'm really glad to see you, Travis."

He looked at me with his big, green eyes, put the bag on the floor and wrapped his arms around me, whispering in my ear, "I counted the days until you came home, Ana."

I wasn't expecting him to say anything like that, but it made my insides tingle. He reached down and

Chapter 8

picked up my bag again and that's when Mom and Jim walked up to us. They both gave me a hug.

"I'm so happy you're home, Ana." Mom said with tears in her eyes. "Are you hungry?" Ana exclaimed with her hands rubbing her tummy, "I'm famished!"

"Travis, would you like to go with us to grab a bite to eat?"

"I've already eaten, but I'd like to go with you and maybe have some dessert."

We decided to go to Red Robin, a restaurant where Jim enjoyed having hamburgers. We were seated fast and ordered our food. While we waited, Jim asked how my trip to Portland went. I told them all about Christmas, the girls, how they had grown, and how the time there went by extremely fast. I explained to them how it seemed as if we were always busy doing something. I heard Travis say, "It seemed to me you were never coming back." He didn't realize how right he could have been, but I didn't think it was a good time to tell them everything just now.

Chapter 9

It was nice getting back into a routine and seeing all my friends again. Pam was the only one I told about my dad wanting me to move back to Portland. She was so glad I didn't want to move back there. She was also amazed how Dad had softened his heart before I came home. Winter in Boise was harder than I remembered its being, when I lived here before. It seemed as if there was more snow and much colder. My church youth group went sledding to a place in the mountains near Boise called Hill Top. The hill we were sledding on is across the highway from a restaurant called Hill Top Café. We had loads of fun hiking with our tubes up and down the hill. Travis brought a tractor tube, which was huge. It was hard to get it to the top, but we managed. I enjoyed it the most when four or five of us went down together. We flew down the snow-covered hill. It felt as if we were airborne,

Chapter 9

hitting a big bump someone had built from piling up the snow. It was a wonder none of us got hurt and we left with only a few bumps and bruises. After we were all finished, Mike our counselor, handed us all big cups of hot chocolate. It tasted great after being so cold and wet.

The days of winter seemed to pass quickly and turned into spring. Boise is well known for being called "The City of Trees". We are surrounded by desert, except for the mountains towards the north. The city was aglow with blossoms and flowers. It was the most beautiful spring I had seen in Boise in a long time. Travis asked me to go rollerblading with him. I had never done it before, and I didn't know if I could do it without making a fool of myself. I agreed to try it, and Travis promised he would help me as much as he could. We went down to the Greenbelt, which is a path that runs along the Boise River. We rented some rollerblades and walked to a nice level place to try them out. Travis held on to me at first and after awhile he let go of me, so I was going on my own. I did well on my own for a while and then suddenly, I fell right on my rear end. Travis came over to me and asked if I was all right. I started laughing and Travis put his hand out to help me, but when he pulled my hand he fell on his rear end. We both started laughing uncontrollably, not able to get up for awhile. Finally, Travis was able to get up and then helped me to get up as well.

There was a picnic table close by, so we went over and sat down to check out if we had any wounds. I had a slight scratch on my arm and Travis came out of it with not even a single scratch. We decided he was much better at falling than I was. As we sat there together, I played with the cross hanging around my neck that Travis had given me for Christmas. He asked me if I liked my cross.

"Oh! I love it! Didn't I ever tell you how much I like it?" I asked. I decided I would tell Travis about my dad wanting me to move back home with him. I don't know why I was so nervous about telling him, but I was. I watched his face as I spoke, and his expression was lifeless. I thought maybe he would be upset about me thinking I might move back to Portland with my dad. When I finished telling him, I paused to see the expression on his face, but it was still the same

Chapter 9

undoubting expression. I asked him what he thought, and he began to smile slightly.

Suddenly, he said, "Wow!"

"What do you mean with, wow?"

He then began to explain to me what he was thinking. He told me before I went to see my dad at Christmas he was reading his Bible when a thought entered his mind about me. He told me he felt something bad was going to happen to me. He didn't know what it was, but he decided he would leave me in God's tender care, and so he prayed for me. He told me I didn't say anything about having any problems when I got back, so he thought maybe he had been worried about nothing. "So now I understand why God had me pray for you, wow." Travis said.

I explained to Travis I had been completely uncertain in knowing what to do. The cross around my neck reminded me about that night before I told my dad I was going back home and the turmoil I was in. It also reminded me about the life I had in Boise, and that I wouldn't have the same life in Portland as I had here. The cross was the answer I had needed at the time. Travis told me when he was looking for a Christmas present for me he couldn't decide on a sweater Pam had told him about, or the cross he had seen earlier. "It was as if I had to buy the cross. Now I know why," Travis explained. We looked at each other, leaned towards each other and hugged. We both understood that God was always going before us, preparing the way for us.

Easter was fast approaching, and it was an exciting time for me because it was my first Easter being a Christian. I decided I wanted to be baptized on Easter and when I talked to my pastor about it, he said that was a great idea. So, my baptism was scheduled for Easter Sunday. As it turned out, there were other kids from my youth group, who were going to be baptized on that day as well. The youth group also had an Easter Sunrise Service, which is very early on Easter morning. It's usually planned so that the sun will be rising as we come to the end of the service. Usually one of the youth presents the sermon and the rest of the kids help with scripture and music. Travis volunteered to do the sermon and he did a fantastic job. I read the scripture, since I can't sing. We received a lot of compliments on our service. After the service, the

Chapter 9

youth provided a big breakfast as well. We had scrambled eggs, bacon, sausage, toast, and homemade cinnamon rolls. Everyone seemed to enjoy it. Every bit of the food was eaten.

Later, we started the regular service with singing and then it was time for the baptisms. I was a little nervous since I had never seen a baptism before. Travis was very reassuring and supportive. The church has a special place called a baptistery, where they do the baptisms. I was surprised that Mom and Jim showed up. I hadn't expected them to come. I watched, as my friend Jen went before me. Pastor Dave dunked her forward three times, said a prayer, and she was done. It didn't look so hard after all. It was my turn next. I proceeded up to the top of the steps, my heart thumping rapidly. I slowly stepped down the stairs and into the warm water, reaching to our waist. I stood in front of Pastor Dave. He asked me if I accepted Jesus as my Savior. I replied, "Yes." He then dunked me forward under the water three times, which represents the Trinity; the Father, the Son and the Holy Spirit. As I came out of the water for the last time a wonderful feeling came over me, a feeling of joy and pure love.

My hair hung down over my eyes. Pastor Dave pushed it away from my face and prayed. I then went back up the stairs and went to an area to change my clothes. Once in my dry clothes, I went over and sat with Mom and Jim for the rest of the service. They had never been to my church before, and I wondered what they were thinking about it all. It was a wonderful service, at least I thought it was, but to Mom and Jim it may have seemed over the top.

After the sermon, Pastor Dave gave an altar call for people to accept Christ or for special needs. I was sitting there watching a few people go forward when out of the corner of my eye, I saw Jim get up and walk up the aisle to the front. I looked over to Mom, and she also got up and followed Jim to the front. I couldn't believe what I was seeing. They were both standing in front of Pastor Dave whispering to him. I couldn't believe it. I glanced back at Travis, a few rows back and he had a big grin on his face. I knew he saw the look of dismay on my face. The piano was playing softly as they stood there with Pastor Dave. I kept wondering what they were talking about. Finally, they both returned to their seats.

Chapter 9

Pastor Dave ended the service and I grabbed Mom by the arm and asked her, "What were you and Jim doing up there?"

She smiled, and Jim spoke up from behind Mom and began explaining. "Your mom and I decided to recommit our lives to Christ. When we were both young kids, we had been raised in church, but things happened and we both stopped going to church. So, after hearing Pastor Dave's sermon and seeing how you live your life, it reminded me of years ago when I was your age and how much Jesus was part of my life."

Mom jumped in and agreed with Jim. I told mom I never knew they had gone to church.

"Well, I didn't have any reason to say anything about it until now, Ana."

Jim bent down and gave me a big hug and whispered thank you into my ear. It turned out to be one of the best Easters I'd ever had. Later, we went home and had a nice dinner: ham, scalloped potatoes and lots of other food. I then went up to my room.

Chapter 10

As I sat by my window, I thought about the day. It had been such a glorious and happy day. I glanced down at the park. The weather had been sunny and warm. I wondered if anyone was playing there. To my surprise, the same little girl I had seen earlier last year and at the airport was sitting in the sandbox, all by herself. Another little girl and boy came running into the park and as they did the little girl hurried away. I thought how strange it was that she would leave as soon as other kids showed up. Maybe it was just my imagination.

Every night I would look to see if the little girl was at the sandbox and every night she would be there, only when no one else was around. As soon as someone arrived at the park, she would run away. I wanted to go down and talk to her, but how? She would run away as soon as I went to the park. I would

Chapter 10

have to be tricky. Maybe Travis could help me. The next day at school I asked Travis if he remembered the little girl at the park and he said he did. He then asked me why I wanted to know, and I told him about what I had seen, and that I thought I should try and talk to her.

"How do you think I should go about doing it?" I asked.

"Let me think about it and I'll let you know."

After school, as we rode home on the bus, Travis told me his plan for me to sneak up on her from behind a big tree, not too far from the sand box. He asked me if I noticed what time she was usually at the park. I tried remembering if she was there at the same time or not and I remembered thinking it was right after dinner when I always saw her.

That night after dinner was finished, I looked out the window and to my surprise she wasn't there. I checked the rest of the night and she didn't show up at all. Wouldn't you know, as soon as I thought of a way to sneak up on her she didn't show up? After that night I saw her off and on for the next month, and then I didn't see her again for quite some time.

Summer was approaching fast. Travis and I had signed up to take driver's training two weeks after school was out for the summer. After that I was going to Dad's for a month. Travis and I went to class and it turned out that we were both assigned to the same car and class. Pam ended up being in a different class. Travis and I had Mr. Hansen, our government teacher as our driving instructor. I was nervous about driving; I had never driven at all. At least Travis had driven at his Grandpa's farm, ten miles west of Boise. Thank goodness we drove only automatics. There would be no way I could drive a stick shift. We all passed with flying colors and then we all wanted cars. We made a bet on who would get a car first. I asked Mom about getting a car for my birthday in July. She let me know there was no way I would get a car until I had a job and could pay for my own insurance. With that, I knew I wouldn't get a car anytime soon. I was way too busy with church and school to get a job. Oh well, I had never been very good at winning bets.

My birthday was soon approaching and when the day finally arrived, Mom and Jim took me out to dinner. It was my favorite place to eat, The Lock

Chapter 10

Stock and Barrel. After we finished our dinner, Mom pulled out a small package and card from her purse. She seemed to be excited as I opened my present. I tore open the wrapping and then opened the box.

I glanced up at Mom as she uttered, "Hurry up Ana. What's taking you so long?"

She seemed a little anxious as I continued opening it, trying to rip open the box somewhat faster. It must be good, was all I could think. Finally, I looked inside the small box. Inside was a piece of paper. I unfolded it and written on the paper was a message, which read, "This is just the beginning of a treasure hunt. The clue is: go to a place where there are 31 flavors."

I looked at Mom and asked, "What's going on?"

Mom explained. "Well, it's just what it says. You're going on a treasure hunt."

We left the restaurant and Jim drove me to the ice-cream store. When we got to the ice cream store, I went inside. My friend Alley was working there and knew why I was there. She wished me a happy birthday and handed me a piece of paper. On the paper was written another clue. It said, "Take a left on Fairview and go to the place where little kids have fun parties." I thought to myself that it must be Show Biz Pizza. We drove there, and I went inside. My friend Kate just happened to be there waiting for me. She handed me another piece of paper. I opened the paper and inside was another clue. It began with, "Take a right turn on Fairview Avenue and go to a place where you feed the ducks." I thought a moment about where people from Boise feed ducks. At the zoo maybe or I know! At Ann Morrison park! That's it! Ann Morrison Park!

"Jim, take me to Ann Morrison Park, please." We arrived at the park, but where do we need to go from here, I thought to myself. Jim seemed to know where to go because he just kept driving. Ann Morrison Park is one of the two larger parks in Boise.

From the front seat Jim asked, "Where do we go from here, Ana?"

I didn't know what to tell him. As I paused for a moment, Mom could tell I didn't know what to tell Jim, so she asked me if there were any more instructions on the piece of paper. I turned it over in my hand and sure enough there was more writing on the other side. It said to go to the fountain in the middle of the park. Jim drove to the fountain and I got out of the car. There

Chapter 10

was a flag pole and on the flag pole it looked like there was a sign taped to the side. In big red letters it read; This is for Ana only. I ripped it off the pole and read it. "Go to the most Holy place you know and go inside." I knew exactly where to go; my church. I told Jim to go to the church. He didn't argue with me, so I knew I was probably right. I kept wondering what could possibly be going on. We arrived at the church and there weren't any other cars around the parking lot. What the heck is going on, I thought to myself.

I went to the entrance of the church and went inside. I looked around for maybe another clue and didn't see one. I then went down the hall to the social hall, looked inside and still nothing. I thought maybe the clue wasn't what I thought it meant. Now what should I do? I decided to go to the sanctuary where we worship. I opened the big doors and it was very dark until the lights came on and people came from out of nowhere, popping out from under the pews and yelled, "Surprise!" Everybody was there from the youth group and some others from church and Mom and Jim. I stood there for a moment and then people started coming up to me and were telling me Happy

Birthday. Suddenly I realized what was going on. It was a surprise birthday party they were throwing for me. I was instructed to go back to the social hall. I went around and visited with everyone and talked to each person. They brought in a big beautiful cake, which was chocolate, my favorite.

After having some cake and ice cream they had me open presents; some were fun goofy things such as a bottle of bubbles, or a calendar that was from two years previous, which came with a note that read, "I thought you would enjoy the pictures." The pictures were of mountain scenes. Someone else got me a monopoly game and someone else gave me a deck of cards. They all enjoyed waiting for the next goofy gift. There were some serious gifts such as what Travis gave me. He gave me a Christian book he had been telling me about that he thought I should read. After I was finished with all the gifts, Mom and Jim came up to me and told me they had something for me too. I didn't see any more wrapped gifts so I asked, "where is it?"

Mom replied. "It's outside."

By now there were only the kids from my youth group, and Mom and Jim there; it had grown late. They

Chapter 10

ushered me outside and in the middle of the parking lot was a car with a great big bow on it. I looked at Mom and she nodded her head and said, "Yes, it's for you." I couldn't believe my eyes. I stood there stunned and excited at the same time. I walked up to it and opened the door. Inside were the keys. Mom spoke up and told me there might be a little problem I might have to work on. I looked inside the car again and then I knew what the problem was. The car was a stick shift.

"Oh, that's great! I don't know how to drive a stick shift car!" I exclaimed to Mom. She told me not to worry. Jim would help me learn how to drive it. Just the thought of it made me nervous, but at least I'll have a car of my own. It wasn't new, but it was clean and looked good on the outside as well. It was a white Volkswagen rabbit. I turned to my friends and said, "I guess I win the bet after all!" They all laughed and told me they would pay up tomorrow.

Mom drove me home and Jim drove my car home for me, since I couldn't drive it yet. Oh well, hopefully it wouldn't take too long to learn. It couldn't be that hard, at least I didn't think it would be.

As we were driving home, I asked Mom whose idea it was for me to have a surprise birthday party. She told me Travis had come up with the idea. That didn't surprise me at all. He's always thinking of other people. I sat back in my seat and thought about the evening and all the laughter and fun. I thought how awesome God is and how much He must love me to give me such great friends and family. I hugged Mom and Jim, said thank you and good night to them and went upstairs. As I lay in my bed, my mind spun with thoughts of the night and of Travis.

Chapter 11

The next couple of weeks seemed to go by so quickly. It was almost time to go back to Dad's house in Portland. I kept trying to see the little girl in the park, but it never happened. She didn't show up and wasn't at the park at all. I looked for her every day. I really wanted to try to talk to her to see if she would be going somewhere over summer vacation. With my remaining time in Boise, I did a few things with my friends: tubing down the Boise River, playing football, and going to movies. I wasn't sure about going to Dad's, but I thought I should go. Travis told me he didn't think I should go at all. I reassured him that I didn't think Dad would try to get me to stay with him again.

He explained, "Ana, I don't know what's going to happen, but I have that same bad feeling that I had last time."

"Travis, there's no way I'm going to stay with my Dad. Quit worrying." It made me a little nervous, because Travis didn't usually worry about things. He gave me a hug and said he could trust that God always goes before us in all circumstances and He would take care of me. Travis always knows just what to say. I think I'll miss Travis most of all. I didn't tell Travis, but I also had a weird feeling.

The flight to Portland was a little bumpy and I hoped it wasn't a sign of things to come. I tried to think as positive as I could, but the same feeling kept creeping back.

Dad met me at the airport. He seemed to be glad to see me. He told me the girls were excited to see me and wanted to come with him, but they both had swimming lessons. As we were driving to the house, Dad smiled and told me he had a big surprise for me.

"What's the surprise?"

He slowly answered, "Well, I thought it might be nice to go over to the coast for a few weeks."

I was relieved to hear about his surprise. I told him it sounded great. I hadn't been to the coast since the girls were babies. I wondered where we would stay

Chapter 11

and just as I thought it, Dad told me we were going to stay at Cannon Beach in a Bed and Breakfast, right on the beach overlooking the ocean. It sounded wonderful to be able to relax, walk on the beach, and go to all the little shops in town. I turned to Dad and said, "I can hardly wait to go. It sounds like loads of fun. Thanks so much for taking the time off to take us there." Then I realized maybe we weren't all going or if it was just us two going. I asked Dad if we were all going, and he said absolutely. When we arrived at the house, nobody was home yet.

Dad helped me with my luggage and said, "You won't need to unpack, because we are leaving to go to the coast bright and early tomorrow morning."

"We're leaving that early?"

Dad began chuckling, apparently remembering how I used to sleep until noon when I was younger. "I think you can get up early since I'm driving, and I want to beat all the traffic," he explained.

"Hey Dad, maybe you can let me drive a little, since I have my driver's license," I pleaded. Dad reminded me I was in Oregon, where the laws were different, which meant I couldn't drive. I had forgotten that in

Oregon the driving age is older than in Idaho. I told Dad I had forgotten about that little piece of information and I bet he was glad I wouldn't be able to drive in Oregon.

He smiled and began to laugh and said, "Not that you're not a good driver, but I would like you to have a little more experience before you drive the Sunset highway. It can be rather dangerous at times." I think he was glad the law was on his side, for now anyway.

We arrived home and Dad helped take my bags upstairs. He asked me to come downstairs when I got my things out of my bags that I would need for the night. I pulled out my nightgown and toothbrush, set them out and went back downstairs. When I reached the bottom step, the girls came bouncing into the house. They both tackled me at the same time, almost knocking me over. We hugged each other tightly. It was so good to see them. I pulled back to see how much they had grown.

"My, my, I think you have both grown at least two inches since I last saw you," I said in amazement.

Becka instantly came back with, "You look the same." We all laughed.

Chapter 11

Katie asked, "Did Dad tell you where we're going?"

I told her Dad had already informed me and I was excited we would all get to go to the beach. It's going to be so much fun. I can hardly wait. Debbie walked in just as I finished speaking and she gave me a big hug, which made me feel more at ease. She asked Dad to go to the car to get the pizza and bring it inside. She explained since we were going to be gone for a while, she thought pizza would be good for dinner. We all agreed and grabbed one of the paper plates that Debbie put on the counter. We sat at the table and dug into the pizza. It was quite a nice evening sitting around the table talking and catching up. I told them about my surprise party and my new car, new to me anyway.

Debbie finally stood and said, "You know, it's about time we all get ready for bed. We all have to get up early tomorrow."

I told the girls we'd better go to bed and they followed me upstairs. I said goodnight to the girls and we all went to bed. It was an enjoyable evening and I was happy that everyone seemed to be comfortable with each other. I lay in my bed thinking of Travis, wondering how his day went, and thought about how worried he was about me. Now I knew there was nothing to worry about. Things seemed to be just fine. Things were just perfect, in fact. I said my prayers, asked for safe travel and asked God to be with Travis and went to sleep.

I woke up with a jolt. Katie came running into my room and jumped right on top of me. She shook me and yelled, "Ana, Ana, wake up!" Dad came into my room after her, pulled her off me and told her she didn't have to wake me up like that.

Dad said, "I'm sorry Ana, I told her to wake you up, but not quite like that. The girls are excited about this trip and I didn't realize she would jump on you, like that."

I told Dad it was okay, and I understood about her being so excited. He explained we would be leaving in an hour, so if I needed to take a shower I needed to get moving. Breakfast would be light, with toast and cereal. As he turned and walked out of my room, Katie told me she was sorry about jumping on me and gave me a hug, leaving just as fast as she arrived. I hurried and showered, dressed and put my things together and

Chapter 11

went downstairs. Debbie was already in the kitchen helping the girls with their breakfast.

She looked up as I entered the kitchen and said, "Good morning, Ana. Did you sleep okay?"

I told her I slept great until some little monster jumped on me, as I glanced at Katie. Katie slowly crawled under the table and Debbie promptly instructed her to get back out of there. She slowly came out and I explained to her that it was all right, but she better not do that every morning. I tickled her and we both laughed. Debbie said I should go jump on her a few times and then maybe she wouldn't do it to me anymore.

"Good idea." I replied.

Dad was busy loading the SUV. I ate some breakfast, eating fast so I could hurry and get my things. When I finished, I started to go get my bags when Dad came from outside and caught me before I headed up the stairs.

"Hey Ana, I already got your luggage and it's already packed in the SUV." Dad seemed very pleased with himself. I asked him if he needed any help and he said, "I think I already have most everything except for you, Debbie and the girls."

"Wow, you've been busy," I said with amazement. "I bet you were up super early."

Dad shrugged his shoulders to express that it wasn't a big deal. We all loaded into the SUV, pulled out of the driveway, and off we went. It was dark when we left Portland, so I laid my head against the window with a pillow and went back to sleep for a short time, a very short time. Becka couldn't stand my sleeping, so she kept bumping me with her sharp little elbow. I woke up and looked out the window and it was foggy. I turned to Becka and she looked at me and grinned. I couldn't be mad at her with that cute little face of hers, so I asked her what she wanted to do.

"I'm bored," she said.

I tried to think of something we could do that would be fun and then I thought maybe I could read a book to her. She had a bag with her full of books, crayons, and coloring books. It was too dark to see to read, so I had to rethink what we could do. "I know, let's tell each other story's," I suggested.

"Oh, that sounds fun!" Becka shouted out.

Chapter 11

Dad glanced back from his rearview mirror to see what all the commotion was about. I leaned over to Becka, put my finger up to my lip and whispered, "Shush. We need to whisper, okay Becka?"

She nodded her head yes, and I told her I would go first. I started my story with, "Once upon a time there lived an old lady named Mrs. Sourpickle. She lived on top of a hill with the town of Rabbit City below. On top of this hill stood an old tree, and on the tree grew Dunesberries. It was a very special tree, considering it was the only tree like it around. The berries had an unusual taste. They tasted like a cross between a blueberry and a blackberry, but they were very delicious. Every year the town of Rabbit had a pie contest to see who made the best Dunesberry pie. Anyone in the town could enter the contest. People from all around would go up the hill to pick the Dunesberries. Every year, Mrs. Sourpickle would try her hardest to win, but to no avail. She tried everything she could think of. Some people said that was why she was so grouchy. She hated it when people would bring their kids along with them when they picked the berries. The townspeople had a meeting just before the big contest and decided that no matter who had the best pie, they would let Mrs. Sourpickle win this year, since they didn't know how much longer she would be around. So, the time came for the contest and when the judges came to a decision, it was Mrs. Sourpickle who won. Mrs. Sourpickle smiled from ear to ear. She thanked everyone, shook everyone's hand and was elated. The townspeople had never seen her so happy. From that time forward, Mrs. Sourpickle was friendly, and the town renamed her Mrs. Sweetpickle. The End.

There wasn't a sound until Becka said, "Ana, that was a great story." I thanked her and then from the front seat, Debbie agreed with Becka and told me she thought it was a very sweet story. "Ha-Ha, did you get that? Sweet story?"

Then Dad spoke up and said, "You should write that down. You never know, you might become a writer some day."

I really didn't expect that kind of a reaction, but it was nice. The rest of the trip was quite enjoyable. The fog lifted, and we were glad to be able to see the small towns we passed through. I took a little nap as soon as Becka and Katie fell asleep. Suddenly I felt the SUV

Chapter 11

come to a stop and I woke up. To my amazement, we were finally in front of the Bed and Breakfast. It was an older house, but it looked huge. Dad got out and told us to wait until he checked and made sure we were at the right place. We waited, and soon Dad came out and motioned for us to come inside. We all got out and cautiously went up the steps, not knowing what to expect. We entered the house and walked down a long hall into a spacious living room. It had antique furniture and wood floors. To the right was a medium sized dining room, and to the left were some stairs. At the bottom of the stairs there was an older woman. She was attractive and had a special look about her. Her hair was a shiny white and she had a glowing smile. She slowly walked towards us with a slight limp and introduced herself.

"Hello, I'm Mrs. Brown, but you can all call me Gloria." She told us she wanted to show us all around the house. The house was enormous. I wondered why she had such a big house all by herself. Just as that thought came to me, she answered my question.

She said, "I bet you are wondering why I live in such a large house. It's because this house has been handed down from my late husband's family and I couldn't let it go. All my children live away in other cities, so this keeps me from being so lonely. I get to be around people all the time and it helps pays my taxes. So, don't feel sorry for me I'm having a great time having this house as a Bed and Breakfast."

She headed up the stairs and showed us all our rooms. I had a small room of my own, which wasn't what I expected. I thought I would have to be in the same room as the girls. Becka and Katie shared a room. This must have cost Dad a lot of money. I opened my window and there it was the ocean. It was picture perfect. Not far away was Haystack Rock. Wow! This is… no other word could describe it…awesome! It looked as though there was a path that led down to the ocean. On my night stand was a Bible on top of a piece of stationary. I went over and picked up the Bible and read the stationary. It said, "I hope you read what is on top of me because it has a special message written inside for you. Please take some time and check it out for yourself. Read John 3:16." At that moment I knew Gloria was a Christian. I thought there was something

Chapter 11

special about Gloria. She seemed to glow, and now I knew why.

    I put my clothes away in the dresser and closet. I then sat on the bed and thanked God for letting me come to such a beautiful place and meeting such a wonderful Christian friend, Gloria. I went out of the room and went looking for Debbie and Dad. As I went down the hall, I could hear voices just ahead of me and to the right. The voices sounded like Debbie's and Dad's. I paused for a moment; it sounded as if they were arguing about something. I felt bad about eavesdropping, but I couldn't help myself. I stood there in the hall listening. It was hard to make out what they were saying, but I think they were talking about me. Just then the girls came running from behind me yelling, "Ana! Ana! Isn't this place the greatest?"

    I turned and hugged them both. Dad and Debbie came out of their room and asked if we were all settled in our rooms. We told them that we were. Debbie took the girls hands and led them to their room to see if they needed any help.

    I asked Dad if everything was all right and he answered, "Sure, why?"

I explained, "I thought I heard Debbie and you arguing."

He answered, "Oh no, we weren't arguing. We were only discussing some things, like where we want to go for lunch and what we're going to do for dinner, that's all."

It was a relief for me to know I had been wrong and maybe I shouldn't eavesdrop. Not getting all the information can lead to the wrong conclusion. We ended up going to a restaurant in town for lunch. It had great seafood and some great American food. We decided we would walk around the town and explore the many shops Cannon Beach had to offer. The girls had fun looking for treasures and finally we came across an ice cream shop that had a porch around the front. It had cute little tables and chairs to sit at while eating ice cream and watching the tourists go by. Katie had rainbow sherbet and Becka had chocolate with gummy bears all over it. I had my favorite, chocolate brownie. Debbie and Dad shared a hot fudge sundae. It was a nice warm day, and it was great just sitting and relaxing.

Chapter 11

From out of nowhere I noticed a boy coming down the walkway. He was extremely good looking, tall, with sandy blond hair, and big blue eyes. Wow, I hope he didn't see me staring at him. I noticed he went inside and got himself an ice cream and came outside and stood right beside me. Before I knew it, he was asking if he could sit beside me. I answered, "Sure." I don't know why, but I had butterflies in my stomach. I sat in my chair and then he began talking to me.

"Hi, my name is Nick. What's your name?"

I was so surprised I could hardly get the words out of my mouth. "Uh, Ana."

He stood up, put his hand out and told me it was nice to meet me. He sat back down and asked where I was from. I told him about my situation and that I lived in Boise, Idaho. He told me he was from Portland. I told him how I used to live there, but now I live with my Mom and step-dad.

"Oh, that's too bad. I was hoping that maybe we could hang out some time," he said sadly.

I couldn't believe my ears. A guy as cute as him wants to hang out with me? Wow! Dad was watching me like a hawk, listening to every word. I didn't quite know how to respond to Nick. Then he took me by surprise and asked if I could walk to Haystack Rock with him. I knew Dad wouldn't let me go since I had just met him, but I thought I would give it a try anyway. I turned to Dad and asked him, "Dad, would it be all right if I went to Haystack Rock with Nick?"

"Well, I suppose that would be okay."

"Really?" I asked, shocked at his response.

Dad just nodded his head.

Nick and I finished our ice cream. As I gave Dad a kiss, he insisted I should be back in two hours and that they would be at our place. I walked alongside Nick since he seemed to know where he was going. There was a path leading down to the ocean, gradually winding down a steep hill. We reached the bottom and walked on the beach toward Haystack Rock. It's a well-known place to go when the tide is down. The seaside was captivating, and I kept my eyes open for sea shells, but didn't see any until we reached a small pool by Haystack Rock. It was small, but there was a Starfish lying in the pool of water. We didn't talk much until we went all around the rock and then we decided to walk up the beach for awhile. We walked

Chapter 11

to a small cove where we found a large log we could sit on while we talked.

I asked Nick about his family and he said, "Like I told you before, I live in Portland and I'm a junior in high school. I live with my Mom, Dad, two sisters and I have an older brother who lives in Seattle. He's married and has a little girl. Let's see, what else can I tell you? I like to go skiing. I like hiking and I rollerblade. As you can tell, I love to be outdoors. "How about you?" he asked.

"Well, I rollerblade a little, go to movies with my friends and go to church." I watched the look on his face to see his reaction to the church thing, and he didn't seem to look any different. He told me he likes to go to movies as well. I decided not to go into the church thing right at this moment. I looked at my watch and realized it was almost time to get back. I asked Nick if he thought maybe we should head back and he agreed.

We started up the path and Nick turned and said, "Ana, I had a really good time with you today. I wish it didn't have to end. Maybe we could hang out together tonight after you have dinner with your parents."

I was excited at the thought of spending more time with him. I told him I would like that very much. As we reached the top of the hill, Nick asked if I would mind stopping at the Laundromat to see if his Mom was still there doing laundry. I still had about ten minutes, so I told him it would be fine. We walked into a small building and a lady in the back looked up from folding towels and came over to us.

She gave Nick a hug, looked at me and asked, "Nick, who might this be?"

Nick looked at me, put his hand on my shoulder, and answered her, "This is my new friend, Ana." A tingle went down my spine as his hand touched my shoulder.

He introduced his mom to me. "Ana, this is my Mom, Joanne." She looked a bit older than my mom. She had graying hair, was a little over weight and had the most amazing blue eyes. She put her hand out to me as I uttered hello. I noticed her hands had a ring on every finger, even her thumbs. Nick asked if it would be all right to hang out with me after dinner. She paused for a second and asked what we planned to do. He told her that we hadn't really figured it out yet, but we wouldn't be out too late. It didn't seem as

Chapter 11

if she would let him hang out with me, and then right out of thin air she said, "Yes sure, why not?"

"I still need to go ask my dad too," I explained.

"Do you mind if I go along with Ana to ask her dad?"

"That will be fine, Nick."

"It was nice to meet you, Joanne."

She nodded in agreement.

We left and went back to the Bed and Breakfast. Gloria was sitting in the living room when we arrived. She saw us come into the hallway and got up, then walked over to us. I introduced her to Nick and asked her if she knew if Debbie and my Dad were back in their room. She said she saw them come in just a few minutes ago. I thanked Gloria and turned to go find Dad. We went up the stairs and Becka was standing in the hall by her bedroom.

She spotted me and Nick and started giggling. Then she started shouting, "Ana has a boyfriend! Ana has a boyfriend!"

Just at that time Dad came into the hallway and asked what was going on. Becka went running into her room and closed the door behind her. I told Dad what she had done, and he smiled and said, "Kids, they can say the most embarrassing things at the most inappropriate times, right Ana?" I nodded in agreement.

"What are you two up to?"

"Do you mind if Nick and I hang out after dinner?"

Resting his chin on his hand, dad paused and asked, "Well, Nick, are you a trustworthy young man?"

I wanted to crawl under the nearest piece of furniture, but there wasn't anything in sight. Nick didn't seem to be upset at Dad's question and simply said yes. Dad told Nick he could come pick me up in an hour. Nick said he would be back in an hour, then turned and left.

Dad teasingly said, "My, my, you sure make friends fast, little girl. Do you like this guy?"

"He's okay, I guess."

Dad smiled and said, "You guess? You seem to have a sparkle in your eyes when you're around him."

"Oh Dad, I hardly know him." I turned to go to my room when Dad said that he and Debbie had decided we would eat at the Bed and Breakfast tonight. Gloria loves cooking for her guests and we had heard that she is a great cook. I brushed my hair, put on a little make-up and went downstairs. I had beaten everyone

Chapter 11

else down the stairs and Gloria was waiting for us to come eat dinner with her. She smiled at me as I sat down at the table.

"Where did you meet that young man, I met earlier?" she asked.

I told her all about how I met Nick and where we went and how we were going to hang out after dinner. She seemed confused and said she was surprised that Dad would let me go with someone I barely knew. I told Gloria I agreed with her and that I was surprised too.

"Really," Gloria said. The others walked in just then. Gloria said she hoped we liked what she prepared for us. It was an old recipe that was her husband's favorite. She called it Swedish Meatballs. Along with the meatballs she had made mashed potatoes, homemade rolls and corn. It all tasted very good.

I could hardly wait to see Nick again. I tried to eat as fast as I could, hoping that it wouldn't be obvious how excited I was to see Nick. I finished dinner and Dad asked if Nick and I knew where we were going.

"I don't think Nick said where we're going." It didn't seem to bother dad.

"Well, I was just curious."

Dad seemed to be acting a little strange. I would have thought he would be a little stricter. But, oh well, at least I got to see Nick again. Nick arrived thirty minutes after I had finished dinner. It gave me a chance to run upstairs and brush my teeth and hair. I grabbed my jacket, scampered down the stairs and to my surprise Gloria was waiting at the bottom. She had a worried look on her face.

"What's up Gloria?"

Gloria looking intently into my eyes said, "Ana, I'm worried about you."

I didn't know quite what to say to her. "What are you worried about?"

"I just don't have a good feeling about Nick."

"Why?"

"Sometimes I get an understanding from God about someone that they are not quite the kind of person you can trust."

I was a little surprised. "That's funny. I don't get that impression at all."

"Just be careful and keep your eyes open and God will show you."

Chapter 11

"Pray for me, Gloria and I will try to keep my eyes open, but I really don't see anything wrong with Nick."

"I will be praying for you dear."

Nick came into the house just as we finished talking. "Are you ready to go?"

I turned and started walking with Nick toward the door. "Where are we going?"

"I have a surprise for you."

"What is it?"

He smiled at me with that most amazing smile of his. That smile sends me soaring with unbelievably good feelings for him. All the things Gloria had just said to me just a few minutes ago went right out the window. He took hold of my hand and led me down the sidewalk, then turned on a path leading to a gazebo overlooking the ocean. The gazebo was lit up with Christmas lights strung around the top. The sight was breathtaking. Inside the gazebo was a swing that could hold only two people. It all felt like a fairytale. We sat on the swing and watched as the sun sank slowly into the horizon. Neither one of us said a word. Nick reached for my hand. I hoped he didn't feel the tingle that ran though me, as his hand touched mine. How could anyone think badly of Nick? He seemed so nice. It was a glorious sight, watching the sun go down. After it had gone all the way down, Nick asked if I wanted to go get some ice cream. I told him that sounded great. Nick pulled a flashlight out of his pocket to help us see our way back to town. He held my hand as we walked.

When we reached town, we made our way over to the ice cream shop. As we got to the porch, there appeared to be a crowd of people standing in line for ice cream.

"I wonder why there are so many people here tonight."

"It must be some of the kids from the Christian camp just outside of town."

"Oh, I didn't know there was a Christian camp around here."

"Ya, it's been here for years." Nick seemed to be a little upset. "Maybe we should go. With this line, it's going to take forever to get our ice cream."

"Oh, that's okay. We can go do something else." I said reluctantly. "Hey, why don't we go back to the Bed and Breakfast and see if Gloria can fix us some hot chocolate?"

"That sounds like a good idea."

Chapter 11

I was glad we were getting hot chocolate instead of ice cream after all. It had gotten chilly outside and I was a little cold. We made our way back to the Bed and Breakfast and went inside. Gloria was in the sitting room, watching TV. She looked over at us as we came up the hallway. She asked if she could get anything for us, just as if she knew what I was about to ask.

"Would you mind making us some hot chocolate?"

"Oh, I don't mind at all! That sounds like a great idea," Gloria exclaimed, rising from her chair. "In fact, I think I'd like some too."

We sat on the love seat and waited for Gloria. Soon, she brought in a tray with three mugs of hot chocolate.

"Now be careful not to burn your lips. It's very hot."

It tasted very good. "So, what did you kids do this evening?"

I told her what we did as we carefully sipped our hot chocolate. "We were going to get ice cream at the shop in town, but it was so crowded that we decided to come back here instead."

"Well, I'm glad you did. It gave me an excuse to have hot chocolate."

We finished our drink and then Nick stood up. "Maybe I should get going. It's starting to get a little late and my mom might be worried about me. You know how moms can be."

Gloria and I both nodded in agreement. I stood up and walked Nick down the hall to the door. He leaned over and gave me a hug; my heart raced as he touched me.

He whispered in my ear, "Let's hook up tomorrow, okay?"

I nodded my head in agreement as he looked deep into my eyes. Then suddenly he was gone. I walked back down the hall and Gloria was waiting for me. She asked me if she could talk with me a minute before I went upstairs.

"I was wondering if you're a Christian, and if your parents are Christians as well?"

I wasn't expecting her to ask me those questions and it caught me off guard. I really hadn't talked to Gloria about being a Christian or my parents not being Christians. I told Gloria my story from the courthouse in Boise and went on to explain about Dad and Debbie. Gloria seemed to be surprised and amazed by my story

Chapter 11

and that I had agreed to accept Christ as my Savior. I explained to her that the day of the court hearing I was so upset when Dad yelled at Mom and Wanda was so easy to talk to, and so understanding. "I think she sympathized with me because her son was the same age as me. Quite frankly, I would have done anything at that point. I was so upset, and God gave me Wanda."

Gloria asked if I knew Wanda's last name and I told her I didn't, wishing sometimes I had. "I'm glad she came back to me and talked to me about God. It changed my life. I was hoping to run into her somewhere in Boise sometime, but I haven't yet."

Gloria stood there in disbelief.

"I know it all sounds strange, but it really happened like I said."

Gloria walked up to me, wrapped her arms around me and whispered in my ear, "I'm glad Wanda listened to our Heavenly Father. You are so sweet."

I whispered back, "So are you Gloria, and keep praying for me, would you?"

Gloria leaned back and looked into my eyes; as if to let me know she was the real deal as far as a

Christian goes. "I already have and will continue to pray for you and your family," replied Gloria.

I thanked her and went upstairs. I went to my parents' bedroom and paused before tapping on the door. I wasn't sure if I should bother them or if they were already in bed. I heard Dad ask me to come on in. I opened the door and Dad was on his feet walking towards me. Debbie was sitting on a little loveseat like the one in my room.

"Hi honey! How was your date? Did you have fun?"

I told Dad about my night with Nick and he asked me if I liked Nick. I was surprised; Dad seemed as if he wanted me to like Nick and acted excited about Nick. "I might like him a little."

Dad jumped in and said, "a little?"

His response shocked me. "What's going on Dad? You seem awfully eager to get me hooked up with Nick. Tell me, what's going on?"

Debbie jumped in and answered for Dad. "I think your Dad just wants you to have some fun while we're here. Right... honey?"

Dad nodded his head in agreement and said, "I just want great things for you. I was afraid you might be

Chapter 11

bored hanging out with us all the time, so I was glad to see you met someone your own age."

I paused while I thought about what he had said, and then realized he just wanted the best for me. I kissed Dad and Debbie goodnight and went to my own room. I said my prayers, and my thoughts immediately went to Travis. I realized I hadn't thought about him since I met Nick here in Cannon Beach. I hope he's doing well.

I awoke the next morning to raindrops falling on my window. I got out of bed and looked out the window to see dark black clouds coming into the shore. I thought Nick wouldn't want to come over with all this rain. I felt ill, and my chest ached inside as I came to the realization that I might not see Nick today. I went down stairs for breakfast and I was the first one there. Gloria came out of the kitchen and was surprised to see me up so early.

"Good morning, Ana!"

"Good morning!"

Gloria asked what I would like for breakfast. I thought for a minute and decided on some cold cereal. I wanted to make it easy on Gloria. She had been doing so much for us. She brought my cereal to me and just as I began eating, the phone began ringing in the kitchen. I could hear Gloria's soft voice speaking to someone. Gloria came out of the kitchen and said the phone was for me. I was excited, thinking it might be Nick. I went into the kitchen, which I hadn't been in yet and was amazed at how big it was. It was done in light yellow and white. I found the phone lying on the counter. I quickly picked it up in anticipation of hearing Nick's voice.

"Hello." I was startled to hear a woman's voice. I didn't recognize it and then she told me she was Nick's Mom, Joanne. I waited to find out what she wanted, and she began to explain why she was calling. She said that Nick was on his way over to pick me up. I thanked her, and she said she hoped Nick and I had a wonderful day. Just then I heard a knock at the door. I went down the hall and opened it to see a very handsome guy standing there. It was Nick, dressed in waterproof gear. I could barely see his face peeking out of his hood. My heart leaped as I looked into his striking blue eyes, smiling back at me.

Chapter 11

"Are you going to let me in or do I have to wait outside in the rain?"

"Oh, I'm sorry, come on in," I said as I stepped aside. Nick came inside and shook the rain off his raincoat. There was a nice big rug in front of the door to keep the floor from getting wet.

"So, what are you up to?" I asked.

He looked at me with those sweet eyes and explained that he wanted to take me to Seaside and go to the beach and ride on the dune buggies. "It's a lot of fun!" he encouraged.

"You do realize that it's raining and might be a little cold?"

Nick said he already made a call and found out the weather was better in Seaside.

"Come on, don't you want to go with me? It'll be fun. Have you ever ridden on a dune buggy before?"

"No, I've never been on a dune buggy. But I've always thought it sounded like fun."

"Well, then, come with me. It'll be fun. If you don't, you'll just be stuck here watching it rain all day."

"Alright, I'll go with you, but I need to ask my dad if I can go first."

"I already asked him last night if you could go with me and he said it would be okay."

"Are you sure he knows about this?"

"Yes, I talked to him last night."

"Okay, wait here. I'll be right back."

I ran up the stairs and went into my room and got a heavy rain coat. Just as I came out of my room, Dad was standing at the door, waiting for me.

"Where are you going?"

"I thought you knew where I was going."

Dad began to laugh softly as he reassured me. "I did know. I was just messing around with you. Nick asked me about it last night and it sounds like a lot of fun." He gave me a hug and told me to go have a good time, but to be careful. I ran down the stairs to find Nick waiting patiently for me. Nick grabbed my arm and ushered me outside to his Mom's car. He opened my door for me, then went around to the drivers' side and got in.

As Nick drove away from town, the rain was beating down on the windshield. The closer we got to Seaside, the more the rain started to let up. I couldn't believe it. Nick was right about the weather; it wasn't

Chapter 11

raining at all in Seaside. Nick seemed to know exactly where to go. We went to a building near the beach which had dune buggies for rent. Nick arranged for the dune buggies and a man who looked to be in his forties came out to explain how to use them. It didn't seem too hard to maneuver them and we both got on our own dune buggy. Nick took the lead, starting out slow and then going faster. I was a little nervous at first but then I started feeling more confident in my ability and my competitive nature began to take over. Before I knew it, I was flying over the dunes moving ahead of Nick. It was so much fun. I didn't think I would do as well as I did. Nick caught up with me and I could see the smile on his face as I slowed to a stop to talk to him. As he pulled up to me he told me he couldn't believe how fast I caught on. He said he didn't think I had it in me but was glad to see I liked the outdoors as much as he did. Suddenly, he sped off over the next dune. I tried to go after him, but my dune buggy wouldn't go. I tried to do everything exactly as I had before, but it wouldn't go. Nick was long gone, and I didn't know what to do.

I sat for a few minutes thinking about what I should do. I decided to pray. Just as I started, Nick appeared from around the same dune where I'd seen him leave. He pulled along side of me and asked what was wrong. I explained that my dune buggy wouldn't go. Nick got off his dune buggy and told me to get off mine, so he could see if he could fix it. He tinkered with it for a minute and decided there was something wrong with it that was beyond his knowledge. He suggested I ride with him and go back to the dune buggy rental store. We had to sit close and I could feel the warmth of his body as we rode back. We reached the dune buggy rental store and told the man what had happened. He told us not to worry about it and reassured us that he would take care of it. We made the decision not to go out again. We had already wasted too much time and decided we would go into town to do some shopping and head back home. We went through some of the shops and stopped to play a little while at the arcades. Nick and I played a few games, got a bite to eat and then started home. I sat back in my seat and began thinking of the fun time I had had with Nick. Then to my dismay, I realized I hadn't thought about Travis

Chapter 11

for a while. I started wondering what he was doing and if he thought about me at all. Why am I thinking about Travis when I'm here with Nick, who is good looking and nice, and we have lots of fun together? What's wrong with me? Travis is good looking too, in his own way. He's everything Nick is, but there's something special about Travis; I can't put my finger on it. I looked over at Nick and he looked at me and asked what I was thinking. I didn't tell him the whole truth, only the part about how much fun we had. He murmured back he had a great time as well. He reached over and squeezed my hand. The day had been so nice until we started nearing Cannon Beach. The fog began rolling in, making it hard to see. I usually don't get very nervous, but I could tell Nick was having a hard time seeing. I wondered what Travis would do at a time like this. I answered my own question. I knew exactly what he would do. He would pray, and he would stay calm. Nick seemed to be white-knuckling it. We were getting close to the Bed and Breakfast and I was relieved when we finally pulled into the driveway. I almost felt him breathe a sigh of relief as he put the car in park.

He sat quietly for a moment before he turned in his seat, leaned over and before I knew it, his lips were touching mine. It was my first kiss, and it kind of startled me. Nick could tell I was startled and pulled away and apologized. I let him know it was okay, and then I opened the car door and got out. Nick got out of the car and came around to me and stood in front of me.

"Ana, I like you a lot. You're fun to be around, you're easy to talk to and you're pretty."

I didn't know what to say, except to answer back and let him know I liked him too. He leaned down and kissed me again. His lips were soft, and this time lingered a little longer. He reached up and touched my face lightly with his hand. "Ana, do you want to do something tomorrow?"

"Sure," I said giving him a hug.

I went inside and found Dad waiting for me. He gave me a hug and informed me how worried both Debbie and he had been about me. I knew why they were worried and didn't blame them. I had been worried too. I let Dad know Nick was a very good driver and there was nothing to worry about. "I'm sure Nick is a good

Chapter 11

driver, but even good drivers have a hard time seeing in the fog, especially when it's raining."

I didn't dispute what he was saying, but there wasn't anything I could do. We had to come home. Dad dropped the subject and went on to tell me we were having dinner in a few minutes, so I should go upstairs and freshen up and then come back down for dinner. I ran upstairs, went in my room and sat on the edge of my bed. I began thinking of the events of the day and Nick's kiss. I'd never kissed a boy before; it was a nice feeling, but am I truly walking in God's will? Why can't this God thing be a bit easier?

Chapter 13

I heard a knock on the door, bringing me out of the nice thoughts of Nick. Then I heard a soft voice; it was Becka.

"Ana, Ana, are you in there?" I opened the door to see a bright smiling face looking at me. She exclaimed, "I missed you Ana! Are you having dinner with us tonight?"

I responded to her with a long hug. "Of course, I am."

She grabbed my hand as if I was ready to go down to dinner and I pulled back my hand. "I need to clean up a little bit first, sweetie. Do you want to sit down and wait in my room while I get ready?"

She didn't waste any time at all. She ran and jumped onto my bed, spreading her arms out wide like a bird as she soars in the sky. Becka cried out with pain, hitting her chin as she landed. I laughed and told her she deserved what she got since she messed up my bed.

Chapter 13

She didn't appear to be hurt; at least there wasn't any blood. I think she just wanted my attention. I washed my face and changed my clothes while Becka asked all kinds of questions about my day and about Nick. I told her about all the fun we had, but I didn't tell her about the kiss. She would probably make it a big deal and tell everyone. It was kind of a special time for me and I wanted to savor it for a while.

I finally finished getting ready and we went downstairs. Debbie, Katie, and Dad were already seated at the table. I took my seat next to Katie and asked how everyone was doing. Katie went on to tell me every detail of her day. She'd had a busy day hiking through Ecola Park with Dad, Debbie and Becka. As she rambled on, my mind kept going back to the thoughts of Nick and the kiss. I could still feel his lips pressed softly on mine.

I realized Katie was asking me a question and it brought me back to reality. I apologized and asked her to repeat the question.

Dad interrupted our conversation, "Ana, is there something wrong?

I didn't want to tell everything about Nick, so I explained that I was just a little tired after my big day with Nick. Dad didn't go into it any further and I was so glad. We all talked about the day ahead. We were going to Lincoln City to do a little shopping at the Outlet Mall. Our meal was great just as it always was; Gloria is a superb cook. We finished our dessert and then I helped Gloria with the dishes. Gloria tried to tell me I didn't need to help, but I continued carrying the dishes into the kitchen. I started putting the dishes in the dishwasher while Gloria put all the leftover food away. In no time we had the kitchen all cleaned up and ready to go for the morning. Gloria was well organized. She had everything ready for the next day. Gloria asked me how it was going with Nick and I thought for a second before I let her know how I was feeling. Thoughts quickly ran through my mind; should I tell all or should I give her the same answer I gave my family? Gloria wasn't like my family. She seemed to know more than anyone how I felt about Nick. I decided to open up and tell Gloria how I was really feeling about Nick. I began by telling her about the feeling of excitement I get when we're together and

Chapter 13

how at ease I am when we are together. Gloria paused, her face without any expression, and I knew without her speaking a word, she was still unsure about Nick. I waited until she spoke and then it came. Soft tender words came rolling out of her mouth. "Ana, I still don't feel Nick is good for you. I can't put my finger on it, but it doesn't feel right to me. I know you'll make the right decision because you are a smart girl. I'm praying for you and I know you'll listen to God."

Tears welled up in my eyes as I reached over, put my arms around Gloria and hugged her. I pulled away and saw a tear in Gloria's eye as well. Neither one of us spoke as I went toward the stairs, lifting my hand to wave goodnight as I began to climb the stairs to my room.

I put on my nightgown and got into bed. I lay there, and the tears rolled down my cheek as I began thinking of what Gloria had said. I began saying my prayers, telling God how much I love Him and then asking Him to guide me with my decisions concerning Nick. I also prayed for my family, Travis and Nick.

The next day it was still raining, and I dressed in warm clothes for the day. I went downstairs and to my surprise, Nick was sitting at the dining room table. I walked over to him and he looked up at me and said, "Surprise!"

I was standing there speechless.

"Are you happy to see me?" Nick asked as he rose to his feet.

I stuttered as I struggled to find something half way intelligent to say. He gave me a hug and then I heard someone speaking behind me. It was Dad. He began to explain that he had arranged for Nick to come with us. I couldn't believe my ears. I hugged Dad and whispered in his ear, "Thanks, Dad."

We had breakfast, gathered our coats and climbed into the car. The girls seemed excited that Nick and I were going with them. I was almost nervous about the girls bothering Nick, but he seemed to enjoy the girls. The time seemed to fly by and soon we arrived at Lincoln City.

We climbed out of the SUV and went into the first store. As we wandered through the other stores, we all seemed to find a few things to buy. The girls wanted everything they saw, but Dad limited them to only two things each. They both had a terrible time deciding

Chapter 13

what they wanted. Katie had the hardest time out of all of us deciding what to buy. Debbie ended up taking her back to one of the first stores. After a long morning of shopping, we finished up at the mall and then decided to have lunch. Nick had suggested a seafood restaurant that had good seafood, so we decided to try it. It turned out he was right. The chowder was delicious and so was everything else. Since the girls were picky and didn't like seafood, they both had chicken strips as they do every time we go out to dinner. At least they knew what they wanted. I couldn't believe how quickly the day was passing. Nick told Dad about a good place to see some whales. Nick directed Dad as he drove, taking us closer to the beach. Dad found a parking place and we made our way down to the beach. As we stood there looking out at the huge ocean, Nick stood very close to me. He casually reached out and put his hand in mine. I wasn't surprised to feel his hand; I had been hoping he would hold my hand.

Becka and Katie entertained themselves by running up and down the beach. Thank goodness the rain had let up and the sun was poking through the clouds. The air smelled fresh and the sand was still wet. Debbie had brought a blanket for us to sit on. We sat there watching for whales when suddenly Becka yelled out, "I see one, I see one!" She pointed to the spot where she thought she saw a whale. We all got up to look and discovered it wasn't a whale but a boat. We all laughed and then a short time later, Nick spotted a whale. It was so exciting! Even though the whale was so far out we could barely see it, we all got to see the massive size of a whale and I got to see it with Nick. It was starting to get dark, so we gathered up all our things, loaded up and began the trip back to Cannon Beach. Both girls fell asleep as soon as we started down the road. Nick slipped his arm around my shoulder and I didn't hesitate to lean against him. I didn't want the day to end.

Dad dropped Nick off at his place and then hurried home because he knew Gloria was waiting for us with our dinner. She had made one of my favorite dishes, spaghetti. I love spaghetti, especially the way Gloria makes it. She puts lots of meat in the sauce, which makes it thick, and lots of mushrooms. We told Gloria about our amazing day and the whales we spotted out

Chapter 13

in the ocean. After dinner, the girls went upstairs for a bath and Debbie put them to bed.

Dad stayed downstairs with me and we sat at the table and talked for a while. He started asking questions about Nick. "Do you like Nick? Are you getting serious about him?"

I was surprised by his questions and wasn't quite sure what to tell him. I liked Nick well enough, but I wasn't quite sure what Dad was after. I carefully answered his question as best I could. "Gosh Dad, I like him, but I am only 14 you know. How serious can it be? He's easy to talk to and I enjoy spending time with him. But that's about as serious as it's going to be for awhile."

Dad seemed disappointed with my answer. I couldn't understand why he seemed to want me to like Nick so much. "I like Nick a lot and it looks as though Nick likes you, too."

I was getting tired and annoyed with this conversation. "Dad, I'll talk to you about this some other time. I'm tired."

"I think you like Nick more than you're letting on," he teased.

I was thinking of how much I would like to talk to Gloria and reassure her about how nice Nick really is. I was disappointed because Gloria had already finished with the dishes while Dad and I talked, and she had gone to bed. I went upstairs to my room and I said my prayers and went fast to sleep.

I awoke with the sun beaming in my room. I opened the blinds and looked out at the ocean, with its amazing view. It was the clearest day we'd had since we'd been there. I got dressed, glad I could finally wear some of my summer clothes. It felt good to put on shorts and a tee shirt.

I went downstairs and into the kitchen to see Gloria. We almost collided as she was coming out to the dining room. She was carrying a tray full of dishes. A collision would have been disastrous, with broken dishes everywhere. Gloria screeched, as she realized I was on the other side of the door. I waited until she entered the room, so I didn't frighten her.

She placed the tray on the table and turned with a look of relief and said, "that was a close call."

I said, "Yep," and then we both began to laugh since everything was safe on the table. I helped Gloria

Chapter 13

set the table and asked if there might be something else I could do to help her. She paused for a moment and then she told me it would help a lot if I could crack some eggs for the omelets she was making for breakfast.

"I would love to, since I love omelets." I cracked all the eggs Gloria had laid on the counter and asked if there was any more I could do. Gloria was surprised I had finished so quickly and commented it would have taken at least another two minutes for her to crack all those eggs herself. She made toast and I helped carry out all the jams and butter. I could hardly wait to eat; the aroma was overwhelming. By now everyone was coming down for breakfast.

"My goodness Ana, I might have to put you on the payroll if you're going to keep helping me so much!" She went on, "Most people don't help out and I don't expect them to, but I'm not going to look a gift horse in the mouth. Thank you, Ana, for helping me. I also enjoy your company. You're such a sweet young lady. Please stay that way, would you?"

I was delighted with what Gloria said. "Gloria, you're a sweet young lady too." We both began laughing. As everyone filed in and sat at the table, I came in and joined them. None of them knew the special time Gloria and I had just experienced together and wouldn't think it as special as we did. We all enjoyed our delicious breakfast.

Dad seemed excited about something. I was wondering what was up and then he told us we were all going to do something different today.

"Where are we going, Daddy?"

Becka chimed in, "What's the surprise, Daddy?"

"Well," Dad began, "every year Cannon Beach has this special event. It's called Cannon Beach Sandcastle Days. There are people who come here from around the area or who live here, who build sandcastles right on the beach. I thought it would be fun to go see all the sandcastles. Does that sound fun?" Dad asked.

Gloria walked into the room to see what all the commotion was about. She soon found out we were going to the beach to see the sandcastles. "Oh, you are all going to just love the sandcastles! There are always some really awesome sandcastles and I know the girls will have a great time!"

Chapter 13

We got our things together, I grabbed my camera and we all walked to the beach. I was hoping Nick could go with us, but he told me he had to do something with his mother today. It would have been great fun to be with him. Oh well, I'll have fun with my family. We walked to the beach and I couldn't believe how many people were already looking at the sandcastles. The exhibits were roped off, so people wouldn't ruin them. There were some magnificent ones and the girls loved them. We had a hard time keeping up with the girls. They ran from one sandcastle to next. My favorite was a polar bear. It was huge, and it must have taken a lot of sand and time to build it. It turned out to be a perfect day for the sandcastles. The sun was shining, and the wind was calm. We had been to every sandcastle and were starting to get a little hungry, so we decided to go into town and have some lunch. The girls wanted pizza, so we went to a pizza joint that was within walking distance. As Dad ordered the pizza and drinks, we filled the paper cups they handed Dad for the fountain drinks and found a booth.

As I walked past a booth, I noticed a couple sitting there together. At first, I didn't realize who it was until

I took a second look. It was Nick sitting in the booth and eating pizza with another girl. I must have stood there for a minute in shock before he looked up and saw me staring at them both. I think he was surprised to see me. Dad walked up behind me and stopped beside me when he realized what I was looking at.

Dad said to Nick, "Oh, hi Nick, how are you doing?"

Nick seemed nervous as he spoke. "Oh, hi you guys, this is my friend Jessica. Jessica these are my new friends I was telling you about, Ana and her family. This is Ana's Dad, Mark."

"It's very nice to meet you."

"It's nice meeting you as well," Dad said as he softly grabbed the back of my elbow and guided me to our table.

I probably looked stupid standing there, not saying a word. Thank goodness Dad helped save me from any more torture. We sat and waited for our pizza. I was glad I was seated where I couldn't see Nick and the girl. Thoughts raced through my mind. Maybe she was just a friend, or a cousin. I realized I didn't have a hold on Nick. After all we've only known each other

Chapter 13

for a short time. We've never said "I love you" to each other, so I guessed I had better cool my jets and relax.

"Are you okay, honey?"

"Yes, I'm fine." I don't think he believed me, but I really was fine, at least for now. Nick and Jessica left soon after we got our pizza. I was quiet the rest of the time we were there, and Dad picked up on my quiet mood. We all finished our lunch and left to go back to Gloria's. I went straight up to my room. Dad followed me upstairs, sat down on the bed beside me and put his arm around my shoulder.

"Do you want to talk about it?"

As soon as he asked the question, I broke down and cried. Dad held me tight and comforted me or tried to. Finally, my crying let up and I began to giggle. Dad said, "That's my girl. It's probably not what you think anyway. You should give him a chance before you jump to conclusions."

I have never felt like this before. My heart truly ached and I hated this feeling. I kept thinking of the girl who was with Nick. She was cute, with long, blonde hair and blue eyes. I wonder if I should call him or wait until he calls me. I'm so confused. Maybe

I should go downstairs and talk to Gloria or Debbie. I sat on my bed and decided a good thing to do would be to go to God and pray and ask Him what I should do next. I began to pray, asking God to guide me in the way He desires me to go. I prayed for all my family, for Travis and my friends. After I was finished, a strange thought came to me. It was that my Heavenly Father was in control and I need not worry. I am with you always. With that thought, I felt much better. God always knows best and even though times may get tough He always helps me through the storms of life.

I went downstairs and went into the kitchen to see if Gloria was getting ready to prepare dinner. Sure enough, she was in the kitchen, peeling potatoes. "How did you like the sandcastles?" she asked as she looked up.

"We had lots of fun looking at them, except we had a hard time keeping up with the girls."

Gloria chuckled and agreed with me. She thought they were probably like two busy bees. Gloria looked intently at me and asked if something was wrong. I paused and decided not to tell her about Nick and Jessica. I didn't want to lie to her, so I told her I was

Chapter 13

a little tired, being in the warm sun and all, which was true. I asked Gloria if I could help her peel some potatoes and she seemed pleased that I wanted to help. I peeled the rest of the potatoes when Gloria suddenly remembered something she had for me. She wiped her hands on her apron and disappeared through the doorway. I waited until she came back, wondering what in the world she could possibly have for me. Soon she walked back into the kitchen with something white in her hand. As she came closer I realized it was an envelope. "I'm so sorry, Ana, I almost forgot to give it to you," Gloria said as she handed it to me.

I took the envelope from her and hurried to see whom it was from. I thought maybe it was from Nick, but to my surprise, it was from Travis. I could tell Gloria was wondering who Travis was, so I told her it was from a friend in Boise. "He must be a pretty close friend if he's writing to you here on your trip. I wonder how he knew where to send it?"

I was thinking the same thing myself. I began to worry a little because I didn't think he knew I was in Cannon Beach. I excused myself to go into the living room, so I could read the letter by myself, knowing Gloria would understand. I sat down and began reading.

Dear Ana,

I bet you're surprised I'm writing to you, and yes, it was hard finding out where you are, but you know how persistent I am.

I giggled as I read and had to agree. He is more persistent than anyone I know. I continued reading.

There were two reasons why I needed to write to you. One, remember the bad feeling I told you I had before you left Boise? Well, it has increased, and I just want to know if everything is okay with you. Two, remember that little girl at the park? I was finally able to talk to her briefly. At least now she doesn't run away when I show up at the park. She still hasn't talked to me, but maybe when you come home she will talk to you, since you're easy to talk to. Anyway, as for me, Ana, I miss you a lot and I hope everything is going well for you. I hope I haven't been too much of a downer, that wasn't my intention. I just want you to know how much you mean to me and I can't wait until you come back home. If you have time, send me a quick note.

Chapter 13

He signed it,

Love, Travis.

P.S. everyone here at church misses you!

It brought tears to my eyes to read Travis's letter. I can't imagine what trouble Travis went to, getting this letter to me. I hope he isn't right about his bad feelings. I didn't realize Travis cared for me so much. Now I'm really confused. I've always liked Travis, but only as a friend. He's not ugly; he's just not gorgeous like Nick. Travis is cute; he has dark brown hair, brown eyes, a wonderful smile and a heart of gold. I went back out into the dining room only to find no one else was there yet, so I went into the kitchen where Gloria was still cooking dinner. She looked up and asked me if everything was all right. I told her about Travis and about my friends at church.

"Travis sounds like a really nice guy."

"You're right, Gloria, in more ways than one."

I heard someone coming down the stairs, so I excused myself and went to the dining room to see who it might be. It was Dad, but he wasn't alone. Nick was with him.

Chapter 14

They both turned as I entered. It was an awkward moment. I wasn't prepared to see him so soon. Nick asked if he could talk to me a minute and I said dinner was about ready and I didn't want to make Gloria hold dinner for us.

"Why don't you join us for dinner, Nick? I'm sure Gloria won't mind," Dad jumped in.

"I'll have to call my Mom to make sure it's okay," Nick said a bit uncomfortably. Dad told him to go ahead and give her a call, so Nick went into the hallway to call his Mom.

"Dad, why did you have to do that?"

"Do what?"

"You know what I mean."

"Oh, come on Ana, give Nick a break. I'm sure Nick has an explanation for what happened today, don't you think?"

Chapter 14

I sat down at the dining room table and told Dad I wasn't sure about anything any more. I guess I could have left, but I just sat there. Nick returned and told us he could stay for dinner if it's okay with Gloria. Dad went into the kitchen to ask Gloria if Nick could join us for dinner.

Nick came up behind me and put his hand on my shoulder. "Ana, are you okay?

As he touched me a shiver ran through me making it hard to be mad at him. I told him I was glad he was here. We ate dinner and then Nick and I decided to go for a walk on the beach.

We made our way down to the beach and found a spot on the sand where we sat in silence for a little while. Then Nick reached over and held my hand. He softly rubbed my hand. Nick began telling me how much I meant to him.

"So, who's Jessica?"

He paused for a moment and told me Jessica was a daughter of a friend of his mom's. Her friend has wanted me to take her out for some time. "I didn't want to, Ana, but she kept bugging my mom about it. I told mom I would take her out for pizza. I really didn't want to since I was kind of, let's see, how should I put it?" Taking a deep breath, Nick looked deep into my eyes. "I guess I'm having feelings for you, Ana, which I didn't expect to have so soon." He continued explaining that he didn't think my family would go to the same place for lunch as him and Jessica.

"Do you like Jessica?"

"Well, she's nice and everything, but I don't feel as comfortable with her as I do with you." He said that he told Jessica about me and she felt bad that my Mom put so much pressure on me to take her out. Nick continued, "She told me she had a boyfriend back home whom her Mom doesn't like, and she was hoping I would take her mind off him." He turned my head with his hand. "Do you believe me, Ana?"

We were looking into each other's eyes and my heart seemed to be beating so fast it felt as if it would fly out of my chest. Nick leaned close and softly touched his lips to mine. I was so overcome with emotion, I found myself returning his kiss. It seemed to last forever, then he leaned back to look into my eyes. I heard him whisper "Ana, I think I'm falling in love with you."

Chapter 14

I was in such a daze; it took a minute before I realized what he had said. I was surprised to hear him saying those words. I didn't know what to say.

Nick put his finger on my lips and whispered, "You don't have to say anything right now, but I just couldn't hold my feelings back any longer." Before I could say or do anything, his lips were touching mine again for a short, sweet kiss. Then he stood up, pulling me to my feet, grabbed me and held me close and kissed me again. We parted and realized it was getting dark, so we made our way back to the Bed and Breakfast before it got any darker.

The sky was ablaze with red and orange. It was a beautiful sunset. Nick took me to the front door, then gave me a kiss and told me he would see me tomorrow. "I'll give you a call in the morning, if that's okay."

I gave him a hug and whispered in his ear, "I can hardly wait."

When I got inside, Dad was waiting for me in the living room. He rose to his feet when he heard me come into the room. "How did it go?"

I told him what Nick had told me and Dad said he knew there had to be a logical explanation.

"I told you it wasn't what you thought."

I agreed with him and said he was right. I gave Dad a hug and went upstairs to bed.

I felt as if I was on cloud nine. I went to the window and looked out to see that the sun hadn't quite gone down yet. It was still red and orange, but a little purple was now mixed in; it was amazing. As I stood there watching the sun go all the way down, my thoughts began drifting to Travis. I couldn't get him out of my mind. There I was, twenty minutes earlier, with Nick, kissing and hugging him and now I'm thinking about Travis. "What's wrong with me?" I put my hands up to my face covering my eyes. I couldn't figure out what was going on with me. I could see Travis's face, his image engrained in my mind. I cried out and asked God, "what are you doing?" The strangest thing happened after I cried out. I looked out into the sunset and saw Travis's face in the sky. What did it all mean? I decided I needed to keep my eyes open about Nick and not let my emotions control me. I got ready for bed, read my Bible for a while, then said my prayers and got into bed and went to sleep.

Chapter 14

My night was a restless one, with the most incredible dream. I was inside a dark cave, the kind of cave that is total darkness and you can't see anything. At first, I was scared and then I could see a small light ahead of me. I began walking and sometimes I would stumble over a rock or a log. I kept on walking no matter what I stumbled over. The light began to get brighter every time I would stumble, and it hurt worse every time I stumbled. Finally, I reached an opening and I looked out of the cave and below me was a path. I followed it until it came to a river. On the other side of the river was Travis. He was waving for me to come over to his side, but the river was too deep. I looked up and down the river, but I couldn't see any way to cross. I felt so confused. Then I looked at Travis again and suddenly a bridge appeared. I walked across, and Travis asked me what had taken so long. He leaned down and kissed me, and it felt as if I was home. I woke up and couldn't go back to sleep. The rest of the night I kept thinking about the dream. Did it mean something? Was it a sign from God or was it just a dream? I finally fell back to sleep and woke up with the sun shining on my face. I got up, took a shower and went downstairs. I was hoping I could talk to Gloria and get her thoughts about my dream. It was early yet and nobody else was up. Upon entering the kitchen, I discovered that Gloria was already in the kitchen working on food for the day and was surprised to see me.

"Oh, Hi Ana. Why are you up so early?"

"I was hoping I could get your opinion about something."

She said she would be glad to help me if she could. I explained what happened the night before and told her about my dream. She stood there, and I waited to see what she thought. She finally began by telling me she didn't feel Nick was the one for me. She also believed God was trying to tell me which guy was for me. "That's what your dream meant. Being in the dark is you being with Nick, and all the stumbling is your time with Nick. And going into the light and seeing Travis was obvious."

It sounded good, but I still wasn't sure about Nick. I still enjoyed being with him. Gloria reminded me it had to be my decision which way I chose to go. "But it's so hard, Gloria. My heart says Nick, but my head says Travis."

Chapter 14

"Ana, tell me, does Nick believe in God or go to church?" asked Gloria.

"I don't know. We haven't actually talked about it." I knew Gloria was right, but I didn't know if I could make the right choice or not.

Gloria sighed. "The only thing you can do is pray about it." She reached over, took my hand and began praying. "Dear heavenly Father, Ana and I come before you with humble hearts. We thank you for your love and for your son Jesus. Ana is at a crossroad in her young life and I'm asking you to help guide and direct her with her decisions. Father God, I care for Ana, and I know how hard this is for her, but greater is He that is in us, than He that is in the world. We put our trust in you Lord, in all things. In Jesus name. Amen."

It was so touching to me that Gloria took time out of her busy morning to pray with me. "Thank you, Gloria," I said as I gave her a hug. "Is there anything I can help you with?" She wiped her hands on her apron and said she was all finished for now. She explained that she couldn't sleep very well last night, so she decided to get up at four-o'clock this morning. She got everything done for the day, as far as the food was concerned. If I had gotten up that early, I would need a nap for sure. I don't think I would get up that early anyway. I went into the dining room and everyone was coming down the stairs for breakfast. Dad asked me how I was doing.

"I'm doing fine, Dad."

He smiled at me and took a seat at the head of the table. We ate our breakfast of pancakes and bacon. It was as good as always. Gloria had all kinds of syrup: strawberry, blueberry, blackberry and good old maple. Gloria always went the extra mile to make everyone happy. The girls loved her pancakes. I've never seen them eat so much. I think they tried each of the syrups on one pancake. Gloria told us she had made the syrups from scratch, and hoped we liked them. Gloria is an amazing cook. I hope I will be able to cook as well as Gloria someday.

"So, what are we going to do today, Dad?"

"Well, what would you like to do?"

I thought for a minute and then said, "I was wondering if we might fly some kites on the beach." I had seen people on the beach, out my window flying

Chapter 14

them, and it looked like fun. I thought the girls would have a blast.

"That sounds like a great idea, Ana."

The girls screamed with excitement. We finished breakfast and Dad suggested we hurry and get ready for flying kites. As we did so, Dad went to arrange for our kites. We waited downstairs awhile for Dad to get back with the kites. Finally, he showed up, but not alone. Nick was with him again.

Nick came up to me and said, "Surprise!"

I was surprised all right. Dad had run into Nick on his way to the kite shop and Nick asked if he could come along with us. I paused for only a moment, and then told him it was okay. Dad picked out a kite for each of us; even Nick had his own kite. We set out down the path, making our way to the beach. Dad helped the girls with their kites and Nick helped me with mine. Debbie was busy getting hers put together. The day was perfect for flying kites. Not too much wind, but just enough for kites. The kite's dad had gotten for the girls were both butterfly kites with different colors, of course. Mine was colorful with pinks, yellows and blues in the shape of a diamond.

Dad and Nick both had fancy kites, with five smaller kites that all flew together. They were the same, except in different colors. Debbie's was quite simple; it had flowers all over it. The girls got their kites up in the air first. They had never flown kites before and they both were doing such a good job. Next Debbie and I got ours up in the air. It was so beautiful to see them flying against the clear blue sky. We had been so lucky with the weather. We hadn't even had much rain, at least so far. Dad and Nick had a bit more trouble than we did getting their kites up. Dad finally got his to fly, but Nick wasn't having much luck with his. He decided to forget about flying it and came over and sat down next to me. He wasn't as patient as Dad.

We sat on the sand and watched the kites flying in the breeze. Other people had the same idea and soon the sky was littered with kites. Nick sat close, his leg touching mine. That same tingly feeling nagged me as we sat there on the beach together. I decided maybe it was a good time to find out a little bit more about Nick's thoughts on a few important areas of my life. I was a bit nervous, wishing he would answer the way I wanted, so I wouldn't have to decide on whether to let

Chapter 14

him go. I began asking him about his parents. "How many years have your parents been married?"

"I think it's about twenty years," Nick replied. "They met when they were juniors in high school." Nick continued telling me about his family and how close they were.

"Does your family go to church?" I held my breath as I waited for Nick to answer.

"We used to, but we moved to a different suburb of Portland that was at least an hour from our old house and we never found a new church. I miss it a lot." Nick became excited when he came up with an idea. "Why don't you move back to Portland with your Dad and I could go to church with you? I don't live too far from your Dad's and we could find a church we both like! Wouldn't that be great?"

Nick had caught me off guard. I hadn't expected him to say anything like that. I just sat there in disbelief.

Finally, Nick spoke up and said, "Come on, it would be great! We could do a lot of things together."

Why was Nick so determined to get me to live with Dad? It almost made me feel uneasy. I began thinking that maybe Nick likes me more than I thought he did.

It might be nice being around Nick more. Maybe I should move back with Dad. Just when I was thinking about that, a girl came up to us.

"Where have you been, Nick? I've been looking all over for you!"

Nick jumped up, grabbing her by the elbow and they both walked a few feet away. Nick whispered something in her ear and then she left. When he came back, he explained that she was a girlfriend of one of his friends. "She wanted to know if I knew where my friend Jake was today."

Nick seemed especially nervous. Maybe I'm just being a little uneasy about things since the pizza parlor incident. When the girl first got here she seemed to be looking for Nick, not his friend Jake. I was still hoping Nick was telling the truth.

We soon finished flying kites and made our way back into town. We decided we should go somewhere for lunch. Nick said he couldn't go with us.

"I have to do some things for my mom this afternoon."

Chapter 14

After Nick left, we decided to get hamburgers and take them back to the Bed and Breakfast with us. We sat at the dining room table and ate our lunch.

Dad asked, "Who was the girl Nick was talking to on the beach?"

I told Dad what Nick had said and Dad asked me if I believed him. "I'm not quite sure."

He reminded me of how I jumped to conclusions the last time and maybe Nick was telling the truth. I still couldn't understand why Dad was sticking up for Nick so much. Maybe he was right though. Maybe I do jump to conclusions.

After lunch, I went up to my room. I decided to read my Bible for a little while. I heard a knock at the door, and I yelled, "Come in!" I was surprised when the door opened, and Gloria poked her head in from around the edge of the door.

Gloria asked, "Is it alright to come in? I would like to talk to you a few minutes, if that's ok?"

I motioned for Gloria to come into my room with a wave of my hand. She walked over to the chair and sat down. I sat on my bed with my Bible in my hands and asked Gloria what was on her mind. She asked how our day at the beach went. I didn't want to get into everything that went on, so I simply told her that it was fine. She began telling me about a special service at the Christian camp tonight and wondered if I would like to go along with her. I didn't have anything planned, so I thought about it for a short time and then told her I would go. Gloria seemed excited with my answer and told me to come downstairs at 5 p.m. so we can have an early dinner before we go to the service. I went and asked Dad and Debbie if it would be all right if I went with Gloria. They both agreed that it would be okay. I returned to my room and lay on my bed and rested until it was time to go downstairs for dinner.

After dinner I helped Gloria clean up the kitchen, so we could leave for the service. I went up to my room to change then met Gloria in the garage.

Gloria's car was an old blue Cadillac, but it looked brand new. She pulled out of the garage and explained that her husband had surprised her for her fiftieth birthday with this car. It was brand new and it only has ten thousand miles on it now. She was glad that he hadn't gotten her a black car, because of the

Chapter 14

hidden meaning behind the color black and turning fifty. "Claude was a wonderful husband. You couldn't ask for a better husband than Claude," she said.

Gloria continued talking about her husband. Gloria wasn't a Christian when they first met while ice-skating, but Claude was. When Claude first saw Gloria, it was love at first sight. He asked if he could skate with her and they were inseparable the rest of the night. Claude asked her out several times and then not too long after they met, he asked her to marry him. "He never missed going to church and would read me the Bible every night. On our honeymoon, the first night we were together, we both knelt down on our knees and he prayed for our marriage and our new life together. I thought it was very sweet, not understanding how important it was." Gloria had a wonderful smile on her face as she spoke of her times with Claude.

"I didn't become a Christian until later in our marriage. I went to church with Claude for years and then one day at church I realized I needed Christ in my life. That was the greatest day of my life and of Claude's life. He had been praying for years that I would accept Jesus as my Savior. I didn't understand what a personal relationship with Jesus was. I had heard about being saved but was afraid of making a commitment. I was afraid God would make me do something I didn't want to do. Then one Sunday I realized how much my Heavenly Father loved me. He gave His Only Son, Jesus, who hung on a cross, and died for me, and would have done so, even if I was the only one in the world. Wow, and all He asks from us is to invite Him into our life. It's so simple, but so hard. I understand why people don't go to church. They are afraid they might have to give up something or change. What people don't understand is He meets you where you are and helps you make it through life's difficulties. We all need help. I wish more people would understand how much God loves us. Oh, Ana, I'm sorry; I get so carried away when I start talking about God." Gloria politely apologized.

    I almost had tears in my eyes thinking about the passion Gloria has when it comes to her relationship with Jesus. I believe Wanda must have had that same passion to have the nerve to talk to a girl like me whom she didn't know, and who didn't know anything about

Chapter 14

God or Jesus. I'm beginning to understand a little bit of how God uses people.

We soon arrived at the camp, where she parked outside a large building that reminded me of a chapel, and two girls came running out to greet us. She greeted the girls with a hug and introduced me to them. Liz was a cute girl with long brown hair and big brown eyes. Laura was short with long blonde hair and blue eyes. They both had smiles that seemed to glow with love. I knew there was something special about them. It had to be their relationship with Jesus.

Liz grabbed Gloria's arm and Laura took my arm and guided us to the place where the service would be held. They called it the worship center and the atmosphere promoted an attitude of worship. It had benches instead of pews or chairs which most churches have. At the front of the room was an altar with a Bible resting on top. There was a big wooden cross on the wall behind the altar. The worship center was so warm and inviting, it gave me an "at home" feeling. People were beginning to trickle in and Liz and Laura went with us to find a seat. We all sat down near the front. People kept coming up to us and Liz would introduce them to us. I couldn't believe how many people filled the center. The service began with music. It started out very lively and then progressed into more of a soft prayerful music. It reminded me of a service we would have at my church, just with different people. I didn't realize how much I missed church and all the friends I had there.

After the service we had cookies and punch. It gave me a chance to meet some of the kids that are at the camp for the summer. Gloria stayed and visited with some of her friends, encouraging me to go with Liz and Laura. They took me around and introduced me to some of their friends. There were kids from all over the country and even some from other countries. After a few minutes, I recognized the girl from the pizza parlor. We saw each other at the same time. She started towards me and I couldn't move. I felt paralyzed. She introduced herself and asked me if I enjoyed the service. I told her it felt good to be in a church again and that I really missed my church back home. She began asking questions about Nick. She wanted to know how we had met, how long I had known him, if we were an item, and if I knew that Nick had a

Chapter 14

girlfriend back in Portland. I was quite overwhelmed by all the questioning. The last question was the final blow. I shouted very loudly, "What?"

She calmly replied, "Oh, I figured he didn't bother to tell you about her." She continued telling me all about the other girl. She told me they'd known each other since they were fourteen and they had been a couple for two years.

I wondered how she knew all this information. I finally got up the courage to ask her how she knew all about Nick's girlfriend in Portland. She explained that the girl in Portland was her cousin, Beth. She was sorry she had to be the one to tell me, but she felt I needed to know.

She explained, "Nick told me that you were his dad's friend's daughter and he was just trying to get you to move to Portland. He told me you lived in Boise with your Mom, and your Dad hired Nick to hang out with you to try and get you to move back with your Dad."

I was shocked. I couldn't even move until Jessica spoke up and asked if I was okay. I still didn't respond. A tear slowly rolled down my face as I thought about

Dad setting me up. Why would he do such a mean thing to me? Liz and Laura were standing there as well. They both put their arms around me, which made the tears stream down my face even more. I felt as if I was in a bad dream and couldn't wake up. It just kept going on and on and I wanted it to stop. What was I going to do now? I was so mad at Dad. How could he do this to me? I was embarrassed by the way I was crying. I felt as if was losing control. Gloria came from out of nowhere, but she came at just the right time. She broke through the girls and asked what was going on? Everyone was silent, and then it was as if she knew what was going on when she saw my tears. She wrapped her arms around me tightly, holding me. Gloria was always a comfort to me and she didn't let me down now. I lifted my head and pulled slightly away so I could see Gloria's face. She wiped the tears on my face with a soft handkerchief, confessing she knew about Nick, but she felt she couldn't tell me because of the situation with the Bed and Breakfast and my Dad. She told me she was sorry, and she tried to give me little hints, but I seemed to be seeing things through rose colored glasses. I knew exactly what she

Chapter 14

meant. I guess I wanted to see things the way I wanted to see them. I didn't blame anyone except Dad and Nick. I was so embarrassed. Everyone was so kind to me, even Jessica.

"What am I going to do, Gloria?"

She held my hands in hers and said, "We are all going to hold hands and pray for you. We call it "being in the hot seat.' That's what we are going to do."

They gathered around me and each one put a hand on me and began praying. As each one prayed for me, my mind wandered to the letter Travis wrote. Travis was right, and I felt like such a fool. I wouldn't doubt it if he was praying for me right at this moment. He is so close to God, which tells me I have a long way to go. I suddenly could hear the prayers that everyone was saying, and I realized God had put these people here for me. He was making sure I made the right decision and making sure I went back to Boise where all my Christian friends are to help me along my life's path. One of my favorite scriptures popped into my head. "If God is for us who can be against us?"

I thanked everyone who prayed for me and asked Gloria to drive us back to the Bed and Breakfast. We drove in silence. It was as if Gloria knew I needed it. We pulled into the garage and got out of the car. As we went inside, we both looked at the clock and looked at each other in surprise as we realized how late it was. It was 10:30 p.m. We knew everyone was in bed and asleep by now. I was relieved I could get some sleep before I had to talk to my Dad. Gloria asked if I would like a bite to eat before I went to bed since I hadn't eaten any dinner, but I didn't feel hungry at all. I told Gloria thanks for all her help and she gave me a hug and whispered in my ear, "Now don't you worry. Everything will be all right."

I whispered back to her that I knew it would be okay.

CHAPTER 15

I slept well considering what lay ahead of me. I woke up and the sun was shining. I decided I would take a walk on the beach since nobody was up yet, except maybe Gloria. I went into the kitchen and sure enough, she was starting to prepare breakfast already. I let Gloria know I was going to go to the beach and she told me to be careful. It looked like it would be a clear and sunny day. I couldn't believe how great the weather had been since we'd been here at Cannon Beach. I found a nice place to sit and looked out at the incoming waves. I sat there with my legs drawn up to my chest, thanking God for taking care of me and helping me find out about Nick. I didn't know what to do. Just thinking about what he did made me so mad. The waves came crashing onto the beach. It seemed to roar louder and louder. I listened, and it was as if God's voice was talking to me in the roar of the waves.

I thought I heard God's voice saying to me, "Be still and know I am God." I heard it over and over until I yelled back at the waves. "What are you trying to tell me?" I waited a minute for an answer, but I heard nothing but the pounding of the waves. Maybe I was hearing things. Just then God's voice told me to say nothing about Nick to my Dad. I couldn't believe God would have me do absolutely nothing. I knew then it was what I needed to do because it had to be from God. In the past my ways of dealing with problems was yelling and getting very angry. Only God would have me do it this way.

I decided to talk to Gloria and see what she thought about being still. I walked back to the Bed and Breakfast and went into the kitchen. Gloria looked up as I entered and asked me how I was doing. I explained what had happened at the beach. She said it sounded like something God would tell me. She went on to say, "God's ways aren't necessarily our ways. I guess that sounds like what you should do." Gloria asked if she could pray for me and I said sure. She began praying, "Dear Heavenly Father, thank you for your guidance. Thank you for your love. I ask you to continue helping

Chapter 15

Ana with the decisions she will be making in her life. She is your child and wants to follow your leading and your teaching. Lord, keep her strong and keep her safe." She ended her prayer by saying, "I ask all these things in Jesus' name, Amen."

I stayed and helped Gloria with breakfast. Everyone started coming down to eat and Dad was the last one. I was a little nervous about what I was going to say, but I knew God would help me. We all sat at the table just as we always did. Gloria brought out our food. She had made pancakes and sausage this morning.

"What would everyone like to do today?"

After some discussion, everyone said they wanted to go to the beach.

"Do you have any plans for today, Ana?"

"I think I'd like to hang out with the family today."

Dad looked puzzled. "Are you doing anything with Nick today?"

I took a bite of my pancakes and shook my head no.

"Why aren't you going somewhere with Nick?"

I explained I would rather do something with the family instead. I quickly added, "Don't you want me to be with the family?"

Dad seemed to be confused and bewildered. "Sure, I want you around; I thought you really liked Nick, don't you?"

Here we go. It's time to tell Dad that I don't care about Nick as much as I did when I first met him, and that was exactly what I did. I took a deep breath and told him, "I think made a mistake and I don't feel the same for Nick like I did before." I think he was totally caught off guard. He looked shocked and bewildered, like how I felt last night. I also told Dad I didn't want to see Nick at all. I had to hold back my laughter, watching Dad try to figure out what had happened with me and Nick. I told Dad I was too young to get that serious about a guy anyway. Dad was stunned and could hardly talk. I finished my breakfast and asked to be excused, when Dad murmured, "Yah, sure."

I ran upstairs and went to my room. I thanked God for helping me get through such a tough situation. I didn't think I could do it and it was easier than I could have ever expected. I hoped it was the end of Nick.

We all went to the beach and Debbie and I sat on a blanket while Dad helped the girls build a sandcastle.

Chapter 15

Debbie sat there for quite awhile before she asked the dreaded question. "Why don't you like Nick anymore?"

I simply answered back, "I just don't want a serious relationship right now."

Debbie didn't ask anymore questions. It was fun watching the girls and Dad making a sandcastle. It was like a work of art. It was kind of like Cinderella's castle. After they were finished Debbie, took their picture in front of the beautiful castle. We thought they were walking back to us, when the girls suddenly turned around and jumped right in the middle of the sandcastle, destroying it all. I'm sure it was Dad's idea. The girls were covered with sand from head to toe. We decided to go back to Gloria's and clean up, then go into town and have some lunch. We went down the hall and into the living room and there stood Nick. My heart leapt to my throat and I finally got out the words, "Hi, Nick."

He asked if I wanted to go into town and have lunch with him and I explained that I was going with my family. Dad came up behind me and interrupted, "Oh, Nick can come along with us." I didn't know what to say. I didn't want to be rude. I walked closer to Nick and whispered in his ear, "I know about your girlfriend and you'd better leave now. And by the way, don't bother telling my Dad I know." I stepped back, and Nick made an excuse that he had forgotten he had to do something for his mom and left. Dad was trying to talk to Nick as he walked down the hall to the door, but Nick never looked back.

I went up to my room and Dad followed me.

"What's going on, Ana?"

"What do you mean?"

"You know what I mean. Why did Nick leave so fast, after you whispered in his ear?"

"Oh, that. It was nothing. Why are you making such a big deal about it anyway? I wanted to spend time with you guys, is that okay?"

That seemed to stop his questioning about Nick and he turned to leave and said we would be leaving for lunch as soon as the girls got cleaned up. I went downstairs and into the kitchen, where Gloria was making an apple pie for after dinner. She asked how things were going. I knew she was aware of Nick's being here, since she probably let him in. I enlightened Gloria and she told me she was proud I hadn't weakened.

Chapter 15

I was glad I hadn't too. Gloria came over to me and gave me a hug and then we heard everyone coming down the stairs. Gloria told me to have a nice day and I turned and went into the living room to join them. We left and walked into town. I truly love Cannon Beach with all its little shops, and everyone seems to be so friendly. We went to our favorite seafood place and sat down and ordered. I was hoping Dad wouldn't bring up Nick while we ate our food, but wouldn't you know it, he did. He asked if I wanted Nick to come over for dinner.

I boldly said, "No!" I guess Dad got the message; he didn't pursue it any further. I asked Dad if it would be all right if the girls went to the camp service tonight, that is, if they wanted to go. They both turned to Dad and pleaded with him to let them go with me. Debbie spoke up and asked if it would be all right if she went along with us. I was surprised she wanted to go. Debbie turned to Dad and asked if he would like to go along too. He made a funny scrunched-up face and I knew the answer would be no. And it was. I asked if he was sure and he said he was very sure. We finished our lunch then walked through some of the stores on the way back to Gloria's. We decided to rest the remaining of the afternoon. I lay on my bed thinking about Travis, wondering how he was doing; was he having a fun summer? I talked to God awhile asking Him if he would speak to Debbie's heart. I didn't know if she ever went to church. That's why it surprised me that she wanted to go with us.

I fell asleep for a short time and woke up to a knocking at my door. I was still a little groggy, and for a minute I thought I was dreaming. There, standing right in front of me, was Travis!

I screamed with excitement, "Travis, what are you doing here?"

Travis smiled and replied, "I came to see you. Why else would I be here?"

I couldn't believe my eyes; I never would have guessed Travis would show up here. I asked if my Dad and Debbie knew he was here and he explained that he called last night and talked to my step mom and asked if it would be all right to come and see me while he was passing through. I told Travis that we should probably go downstairs and talk in the living room. We went down to the living room and I was glad

Chapter 15

there wasn't anyone there, so we could have some time to ourselves. We sat on the couch together and I asked Travis where he was heading. He told me he was with his parents and they were going to see one of his aunts, who lived south of here, in Lincoln City. She had suddenly become very sick and they had to make a quick trip to see her, since she didn't have any kids of her own.

"I talked Dad into dropping me off here, so I could visit with you awhile. I hope that's okay with you," Travis added shyly.

I leaned over to him and wrapped my arms around his neck and hugged him tightly. I gently kissed his cheek as I pulled away and asked how long he was staying and where. I think he was surprised at the kiss on his cheek because his face was beginning to turn red. Travis composed himself and told me he'd be here for two days and he would be staying here at the Bed and Breakfast. I was so surprised but also delighted. I asked him if he had met Gloria and he said he had and he thought she was wonderful. He informed me she was the one that encouraged him to stay here. "She told me she had a small room in the back I could stay in for free. I couldn't turn it down, and anyway I really missed you."

That sounded like Gloria, and I felt a tingle inside me when Travis said he missed me. Just then I remembered we were going to the camp service tonight, so I asked Travis if he wanted to go along.

"I wouldn't miss it for the world!"

Everyone began coming down for dinner and Dad asked, "Who is this, Ana?"

"This is Travis, from back home." I explained everything to Dad about Travis's aunt and how he was going to stay here for a few days. Travis jumped in and asked Dad if it was okay for him to stay here at our Bed and Breakfast. I was nervous waiting for Dad to answer. What could he say? Travis was already here. I held my breath until I heard him say that it would be fine. He didn't sound thrilled, but I wasn't concerned about how Dad felt right now. I was just happy Travis was here. Gloria made another great meal, and with Travis here, I don't think I could have been any happier.

Travis and I helped Gloria with the dishes and then we got ready to go to camp services. Gloria drove us with Debbie up front and the four of us scrunched in

Chapter 15

the back seat. When we arrived at the camp, Liz and Laura were just inside the door. I introduced Travis, Debbie and the girls to them and then we all found our seats. I sat next to Travis and as the sermon began I reached and took Travis's hand in mine. It felt like home, a place I always belonged. The sermon was one of conviction, one of recommitment; the Pastor talked about being closed-minded about God. He read the scripture Hebrews 3:7, "So, as the Holy Spirit says: Today, if you hear his voice, do not harden your hearts as you did in the rebellion, during the time of testing in the desert, where your fathers tested and tried me and for forty years saw what I did. That is why I was angry with that generation, and I said, their hearts are always going astray, and they have not known my ways. So, I declared an oath in my anger; they shall never enter my rest." The pastor spoke about the Israelites and how they didn't obey God and wandered in the wilderness for forty years and not until they began listening to our Father in Heaven were they able to go into the land of milk and honey. He informed us we too can be disobedient. We go along in our lives and we might sometimes think about God, when times are good and sometimes its several days, months or even years before we think about Him. Then something happens in our life, shaking us up. It's then when we turn to God for help. We bargain with God."

"Please help me with this and I'll do better. I'll go to church more or I'll pray more, please just get me out of this mess."

Then the Pastor read Hebrews 3:15, "Today, if you hear his voice, do not harden your hearts as you did in the rebellion." The Pastor went on to say; "We all have a choice to accept Jesus or harden our hearts and never experience the wonderful gift of grace, which is the reason Jesus died on that cross," as he pointed at the cross on the wall.

He asked us all to open our hymnals and join in singing "Amazing Grace". He asked if any one wanted to accept Jesus as their personal Savior or renew their faith, not to harden our hearts and to come forward during the song. We were all standing and out of the corner of my eye, I see Katie start up the aisle and walk to the front of the sanctuary. Then I saw Becka go forward as well. I looked at Debbie and to my disbelief she was also going toward the front. She walked up to the front and stood

Chapter 15

behind the girls. There were other people standing with them as well. I turned to Travis and he had tears in his eyes. He gave my hand a big squeeze and smiled at me. The song finished, and the pastor paused and dismissed everyone who was standing. He began speaking quietly to the ones who had come forward. Travis and I waited patiently for Becka, Katie and Debbie. It took about ten minutes, then they started back and when Debbie turned around, I saw the tears streaming down her face. They reached us and we all hugged. The girls were excited and began telling me they were just like me, a Christian. It warmed my heart to see the girls so excited about Jesus. Debbie was quiet while we listened to the girls go on about the future. I don't think I had ever seen them so excited as this. They both knew which church they wanted to attend, and they were both different churches. Debbie interrupted and told them they would all be going to church together.

Becka volunteered, "Will Dad also go to church with us too?"

We all looked at each other and Debbie was the one to answer her question. "We can ask him and maybe he will go with us."

It made Becka feel better to think he might attend with them. Gloria congratulated the girls and Debbie about the decision they made to follow Christ. Debbie began telling us that when she was a small child she went to church with her parents all the time, until she became a teenager. She quit going and so did her parents. She hadn't been back to church since then except for weddings. She thought about God at times but not as she had when she went to church. Tonight's service reminded her of the love of God and how much she missed talking to God and she wasn't going to make excuses any longer. Also, she wanted her girls to have Christ in their lives. She had a look of peace and joy on her face as she spoke. We needed to go back to the Bed and Breakfast because it was getting late.

We tried extra hard to be quiet when we arrived at the Bed and Breakfast. Dad was upstairs asleep. The girls fell asleep on the way home, so Debbie and I carried them to their room and put them to bed. Gloria, Travis and I sat in the living room and talked about the night. We were all excited with the outcome and knew God had orchestrated it all. Gloria excused herself and Travis and I were left alone. Travis reached for

Chapter 15

my hand and smiled and asked me if I would like to go for a walk on the beach with him in the morning. I squeezed his hand and answered "yes." Travis whispered goodnight and went to his room, and I went upstairs to my room.

When I reached the top of the stairs I was surprised to see Debbie standing there. I thought she had gone to bed. She reached out and hugged me and thanked me again for inviting her to the church service. She asked if we could go downstairs to the living room and talk. I agreed to talk with her, and we tried not to wake anyone. We sat down, and I asked her if there was a problem. She paused for a moment and then she seemed to get the courage she needed to talk to me. I couldn't imagine what she wanted to talk to me about. She started by apologizing and telling me it wasn't her idea. She started telling me of Dad's plan of using Nick to get me to move back with them. I interrupted her by putting my finger on her lips to quiet her. I explained I already knew about Dad's plan. Debbie was surprised I knew and asked how I found out about it. I explained everything to her and how I had decided not to tell Dad what I knew about Nick.

Debbie couldn't believe I didn't let Dad have it with both barrels. I explained that I wanted to do just that at first, but God had other plans in mind. She leaned over and hugged me, and I asked her not to say anything to Dad about what I knew about Nick. She promised that she wouldn't say a word.

The next day came fast, it seemed as if I just went to sleep and then the sun was shining in on my face. I jumped out of bed and took my shower and finished getting ready for the day to come. I started downstairs and saw Travis waiting for me at the bottom, looking up at me and smiling. A tingle slithered down my spine as I smiled back. He took my hand in his and guided me into the dining room where Gloria was putting breakfast on the table for us. No one else was up yet and we both sat down at the table and ate pancakes and eggs. When we finished eating we took our dishes into the kitchen. Gloria gave us each a hug and told us she would let Dad and Debbie know where we were going.

Strolling down the path with Travis reminded me of how I had done this very thing with Nick only days earlier. It looked as though a storm was moving in. Black clouds were on the horizon and we both knew

Chapter 15

we wouldn't be staying long. We found a nice place to sit as the wind blew gently. I felt I needed to tell Travis about Nick but didn't know quite how to begin. I said a quick little prayer under my breath and started. "I bet you're wondering about Nick, the guy I was talking to Debbie about."

Travis nodded his head and whispered, "Go on."

I continued telling Travis about Nick. I told Travis all about him and the plan Dad had concocted to get me to stay in Portland. I paused after I finished, watching Travis's reaction and was surprised with what he said next.

"It doesn't surprise me at all. As a matter of fact, I'm relieved you listened to God and did the right thing. I knew something was happening, that's why I had that terrible feeling. I knew something bad was going on." Travis leaned over and held me close and kissed the top of my head. I was surprised that he didn't seem mad. I asked if he was mad at me and he looked into my eyes and said, "Ana, why would I be mad, you didn't do anything wrong. They both misled you."

I replied to him with as much honesty as I could muster. "Travis, I thought I was falling for Nick. He's good looking and was fun to be with. I even kissed him."

I waited for his response, and then Travis said with such certainty, "Ana, it doesn't surprise me at all. Satan will do whatever it takes to get people to stray away from God. What I see is what I prayed for. I prayed God would be with you and help you through whatever you might be going through. I'm very impressed you did as God led you to do and you found out the truth. So why would I be mad?"

I hugged Travis and he kissed the top of my head again. All at once the sky opened and the rain poured out of the black clouds we had seen earlier. We ran as fast as we could up the path to Gloria's. By the time we reached the house, we were completely soaked. We each went to our rooms and changed into dry clothes. Travis was waiting for me as I came down the stairs. Everyone else was having breakfast as we entered the dining room. Dad looked up at us and asked what we had planned for the rest of the day. I looked at Travis and he said his parents were coming to pick him up later that afternoon. I asked Dad if they had anything

Chapter 15

planned and he said he wasn't sure since it was raining; he thought they might stay in and find something we could all do right there. He turned to Gloria and asked if she had a deck of cards. She said she had a couple of them and she would go find them.

After breakfast, Dad taught us all a card game, called Go Fish. It was an easy enough game that the girls were also able to play. Gloria made us lunch and we played until mid afternoon. We were having so much fun. The day seemed to just fly by.

Soon it was time for Travis's parents to arrive, so Travis went to his room to gather up his things and sat them in the hallway until his parents came. We sat in the living room and talked, just the two of us, until his parents arrived. We heard a knock on the door and I went to answer it. It was Travis's mom, Teresa, who was very pretty with amazing dark eyes and dark brown hair. I asked her to come in for a minute and she explained they really needed to get going so they didn't miss their flight from Portland to Boise. She told me she would see me back in Boise and got back into the car. Travis stood in front of me and bent his head down and kissed the top of my head. I longed to go back to Boise with Travis, but I had a few more days with my family before I could return to Boise. I sensed that Travis didn't want to leave me either.

The next few days passed slowly; it seemed to take forever to finally go back to Portland. We packed our things and Dad loaded up the SUV. It was going to be hard to leave Gloria. She had become a close friend, one I needed at a big crossroad in my life. We all said our good-byes and I said to Gloria, "I'd like to thank you for all your help and for your friendship. I don't know what I would have done without you. I'll write and let you know how things were going." She seemed to light up when I told her I would write to her.

Gloria gave me a big squeeze. As I turned to leave, tears welled up in my eyes. I wasn't sure if I would ever see Gloria again, but I knew someday we would be together in heaven, forever. As we pulled away from the curb, I looked back and saw Gloria standing in the road waving her hand with a hankie in her other hand wiping away her tears.

The drive back to Portland seemed long, as the distance between Gloria and us became further and further apart. I finally dozed off and the girls must

Chapter 15

have done the same since they were very quiet. I woke up as we drove into the driveway of Dad's house. It was getting close to dinner time when I heard a knock on the door. Dad yelled out and asked if I could get the door. To my surprise it was Nick. I couldn't believe my eyes. I didn't ever imagine Nick would try to see me again. He asked if he could come in and talk to me for a few minutes. I really didn't want to speak to him, but I didn't want to be rude. We went into the living room where I sat opposite him. I waited for Nick to begin speaking and it seemed to be somewhat difficult for him to start, so I started it for him. I began with a straight forward approach.

"Look Nick, I really don't have any feelings for you, so I don't know why you are here."

With his head bowed down he said he was hoping I might still like to be friends and maybe we could still hang out together. Boy, he doesn't give up easily or maybe Dad is still trying to get me to stay here in Portland.

"Nick, I think you need to leave," I said as I walked to the door. I think I caught him off guard; he slowly rose and walked to the door. He was still trying to talk as he left. I closed the door as soon as I could without hitting him. Dad was coming into the living room just as the door closed. He asked who was at the door and I told him it was nobody. It really wasn't a lie; it was as close to the truth as I dared.

Chapter 16

The day for me to leave Portland had finally arrived. I was excited to see Mom, Jim and my friends and I needed to get ready for school. I packed my things and said my good-byes to Debbie and the girls. Debbie gave me a big hug and whispered in my ear, "Ana, thanks for giving me an opportunity to find Jesus again." She held me tight for awhile and I whispered that I loved her.

Dad had everything packed up and ready to go to the airport. It was a quiet ride. I wondered what Dad was thinking. Was he wondering why I didn't want to be with Nick or what went wrong? I couldn't read his thoughts, but I guess I wouldn't worry about that anymore. I'll just be thankful for finding out Dad's plan to use Nick to get me to move to Portland. God is good and I'm so glad I made the right choice.

We arrived at the airport and Dad got my luggage out of the car. He seemed a little distant with me. He kept avoiding looking at me, but I didn't let it stop me from giving Dad a big hug, telling him that I love him and that I would call him when I got home. Dad didn't say much, but I did notice a tear he wiped from his face.

I went inside the airport, checked my bag, waited in the long security line and found a seat at my gate to wait for my plane. I pulled a magazine out of my bag and began reading. Suddenly I heard someone say my name. When I looked up, it was a lady from my church at home. Renee was a very sweet lady, middle aged and very pretty. She is the grandmother of one of my friends, Sheila.

"So, how have you been doing, Ana?"

"Oh, I'm very eager to get home to see all my friends."

"I've missed you at church. Sheila told me you were here in Portland, but I never thought I would run into you."

"Why are you in Portland, Renee?"

"I've been visiting my son, David, his wife Kathy and my grandchildren. How did it go with your Dad and the family?"

Chapter 16

I told her about our time at the beach and she was excited about how God had helped me with everything.

"I heard from Sheila and she said that the youth group from church was praying for you."

It pleased me to hear that God was with me throughout my stay with Dad. I bet Travis had a whole lot to do with everyone praying for me.

It was soon time to get on the plane. The flight was smooth and in no time at all I looked out the window to see well known landmarks of Boise like the big company on the east side of town, Micron, and Boise State University. I saw the freeway which meant we were very close to landing. We touched down and taxied to the terminal. Excitement engulfed me as I got off the plane. I walked into the terminal and to my surprise about twenty people had gathered there to greet me. Travis was holding a bouquet of balloons and flowers. Almost all the youth group had come, and Mom and Jim were standing behind the others. It made me so happy to think that everyone had come here to support me. We all mingled around for a short time and then I went home with Mom, Jim and Travis.

I was famished when we got home, so the first thing I did when I got in the house was raid the refrigerator. It felt so good to be home. While mom helped me find something to eat, I told them about my trip to the Oregon coast and all the fun things I did while I was there. I didn't get into the parts about Nick and Dad; it would have upset them too much and probably would have made them angry. After we all had something to eat, we watched a little TV and then Jim and Mom went up to bed and left Travis and me alone.

Travis turned and grabbed my hand, "How did things go after I left Cannon Beach?"

I explained how Dad reacted to my leaving without incident. Travis was surprised he didn't give me any guff. He was relieved to hear things had gone as smoothly as they did.

It was getting late, so Travis got up to leave and then said, "I wonder what Satan will hit you with next?"

This reminded me of the little girl and the sandbox. "Travis, what's going on with the little girl in the park?"

"Oh yeah, she hasn't been around lately. I think she went to stay with her grandmother in Portland again. I'm sure she'll be back before school starts back up."

Chapter 16

"Thank you for watching out for her while I was gone. I kind of feel a little responsible for her. I don't know why, but I do."

Travis kissed the top of my head and murmured as he walked down the steps, "I wouldn't expect anything less from you Ana."

I went to my room and sat inside my bay window. Looking down at the park, I wondered how the little girl was doing and what her name was.

The next few days passed quickly with my getting settled back into Mom's house. On the third day, the phone rang just after lunch. To my surprise, it was Sara, my old friend from when I lived in Boise before my parent's divorce.

"I'm so glad to hear your voice! How are you doing, Sara?"

"I'm doing fine. I was hoping to get together with you and Riley. Did you know that Riley is back in Boise?"

"No, I didn't."

"Yeah, she's back for just the summer and then she's going back to Seattle. Ana, do you think you could go to the mall with us today?" Sara asked.

It sounded like fun, so I told Sara I would have to ask my Mom first, but I didn't see why she would have a problem with me going. I would also need to borrow Mom's car, since I still couldn't drive mine. Mom told me it was okay, but to be home for dinner and be careful with the car. I made the arrangements with Sara as to where we would meet. I drove to the mall and then made my way to the food court to meet Sara and Riley. I was excited to see them and tell them about my new life.

I rode to the top of the escalator and standing at the top were Sara and Riley. "It's so good to see you guys. I've really missed you both," I said as I gave each of them a hug. We decided to have lunch and sit at a table, so we could talk. Sara looked just the same, but Riley was super skinny. She was never fat, just maybe a little plump. Now though, she looked unhealthy. We each picked out what we wanted to eat and found a place towards the back where nobody else was sitting. We took turns sharing what we had been doing since we had last seen each other. I tried to talk about God, but they both changed the subject whenever I did. I decided not to press it. We had a nice time talking

Chapter 16

and catching up. After we finished eating, we walked through the mall looking at clothes. It was almost time for me to start heading home.

"We need to get together and do this again." I said.

"Ana, Riley and I are going to a party at one of my friend's house tomorrow night. Do you want to go with us?"

"What kind of party is it?"

"Oh, it's just a birthday party."

"I'll have to ask my mom if it's okay."

"Cool, I'll call you later to see if you can go with us," added Sara.

When I got home, Mom had dinner almost ready. "Can I help with anything, Mom?"

"Sure, you can set the table for me."

When I had finished with that, everything was ready. I helped put the food on the table and just about then, Jim came walking in and said, "Yum, it smells like my favorite meal, meatloaf." Everything mom makes is Jim's favorite. I was amazed that he knew exactly what Mom had fixed; he was right. Meatloaf wasn't my favorite, but Mom made it pretty good. While we were eating I asked Mom if I could go to a birthday party with Sara and Riley.

"Do you think there will be any bad things going on at the party?" she asked.

"I don't think so."

"You know Ana, we both trust your judgment, so you can decide for yourself."

Sara did call later that night and I told her I could go to the party. She gave me the time they would pick me up and I said I would see her tomorrow.

The next day Travis came over and we decided to meet up with some of our youth group friends and go to an afternoon movie. We went to the theaters near the mall. We decided to go see *Fifty First Dates*, a comedy about a woman who wakes up with no memory of the events of the prior day each morning. I sat by Travis and we held hands throughout the movie. It felt so natural holding his hand. We enjoyed the movie. It had been a while since I had laughed that hard, it was so funny. After the movie, we went to my house and that's when I told Travis about the party. Travis had a strange look on his face as I told him about it.

"What's wrong, Travis?"

Chapter 16

"I don't know. I really can't explain it, but I don't have a good feeling about it."

"You're not jealous, are you?" I asked.

"No, no, no, it's not like that at all, it's something I can't quite put my finger on. Be very careful, okay?"

It made me nervous as well because Travis is usually right about his feelings. He gave me a hug and went home.

It was almost time for Sara and Riley to pick me up, when the door bell rang. I went and answered it and sure enough it was Sara. We went across town to north Boise. It's an older part of town with some beautiful older homes that have been remodeled. The house we pulled up to was one that I've always wanted to see inside of; I guess I'll finally get the chance to now. It was exactly what I had envisioned it would be and even more. It had a gorgeous chandelier in the large entryway. The floor was marble with a large area rug in the center of the floor. We walked down a long hallway which turned into the living room. The furniture was all white; it was so crisp and clean it looked like it had never been used. I think I was right because soon we were ushered into a family room with all leather furniture. The kitchen was connected to the family room with a bar. On top of the counter was a decorated cake with "Happy Birthday, Kara," written on top. I guess it is a birthday party after all.

More and more kids began to arrive; Sara seemed to know them all. She introduced them to us as they came in. I still hadn't met the birthday girl. After everyone had arrived, a beautiful girl with long blond hair made her appearance at the top of the curved staircase leading down to the family room. It was seemed strange; everyone clapped as she came down the stairs. They all seemed to know her. Sara, Riley and I began to move around the room striking up conversations with other kids that we knew. I noticed that the counter was filled with many different foods. It looked as if it had been catered. People came out of nowhere and asked what we wanted to drink. I noticed kids were ordering cocktails, which blew me away. There seemed to be no adults here at the party, just tons of kids. I noticed that Sara and Riley were going through French doors to the outside patio, so I followed them. I realized there was also a swimming pool as well. We took our drinks, (mine was a coke),

Chapter 16

and found a table by the pool and sat down. It was getting more and more crowded. I ate the food I had gotten earlier and watched all the kids. Soon there was a DJ playing loud music. It wasn't the Christian music I was used to hearing.

I needed to find a restroom, so I asked one of the kids and they pointed to the stairs and to the left. I washed my face, looked into the mirror and asked myself, "Why did I agree to come to this party?" Maybe I can get Sara and Riley to leave early. I made my way back to the table and the girls were nowhere to be seen. I sat and finished my coke, after which I began feeling strange. I felt dizzy and light headed. I realized someone must have put something in my drink when I was in the restroom. I just sat in my chair, hoping I wouldn't pass out.

Time was passing, but I had no perception of how long I had been sitting there. It could have been an hour or more. I saw a phone over by the bar. If only I could walk, maybe I could call my Mom or Travis. Why didn't someone see I needed help?

Before I knew it, I was on a sofa with a strange boy. He was kissing me. I tried to push him away, but my arms wouldn't move. I yelled in my mind for God to help me! "Please, Jesus, help me!" Suddenly, someone pulled the boy off me, grabbed me, took me in their arms and was carrying me out of the house. I looked up into that very familiar face that I knew so well, Travis. He put me in his mom's car and drove me to my house. He left me in the car while he went and talked to Mom and Jim before he brought me inside, so that they wouldn't be upset. They all came out and Travis lifted me out of the car and took me inside. Travis laid me on the living room couch. I was beginning to come out of the strange state I had been in and asked, "What happened?"

Mom responded, "That's what we want to know."

I answered back, "I don't know either."

Jim carried me up the stairs to my room and mom tucked me in to bed. I woke up the next morning with the sun glaring through the window. I couldn't figure out how I had gotten into my bed. The last thing I remember was sitting at a table at a party. As I put my legs over the side of the bed and tried to stand up, I was still a little uneasy on my feet. I sat back

Chapter 16

down on my bed and cried out, "Mom, can you come and help me?"

Mom opened the door and sat on the bed beside me. She explained to me about the events of the prior evening as explained by Travis. "We don't know exactly what went on, but we think someone put something in your drink at the party."

"I can't remember anything after I went to the bathroom," I told mom.

After we talked awhile, Mom helped me up, holding me as we walked to the stairs. As we passed the bathroom, I caught a glimpse of myself in the mirror. I looked terrible, in fact like a zombie. Travis was waiting for me downstairs where he had slept on the couch all night. I was walking a lot better. I told myself, "You'll probably feel better if you try to eat something." I went into the kitchen where I found Jim and Travis sitting at the kitchen table drinking coffee. Looking up from his coffee Jim asked, "How are you feeling today Ana?"

"I'm not quite sure yet. May I have a cup of coffee?" I asked Jim as I sat down at the table.

"Of course, you can."

I don't usually drink coffee, but I thought maybe it would help take away the grogginess in my head.

"Travis, why did you sleep downstairs last night?" I asked.

Travis gave Mom a questioning look. Then Mom began to explain. "Last night, Travis was worried about the party you had gone to. He had overheard some kids at school talking about it. They talked about where it was going to be and that there was going to be alcohol and drugs at the party. He was so worried about you, that he went to the party to make sure you were all right. And I'm glad he did. He found you on the couch with a guy kissing you, but you were as limp as a rag doll. Travis was able to get you out of there just in time and brought you home. He was so worried that we decided to let him sleep on the couch. He wanted to make sure you were okay. How could I say no? He had saved you from God knows what. It was the least we could do for him."

I looked at Travis and uttered, "Thanks for being my knight in shining armor."

Chapter 16

I turned to Mom and looked her right in the eyes and told her, "I didn't do this on my own. Someone must have done it to me. Did Riley or Sara call?"

"Sara called last night wondering if I had seen you. I told her you were at home and explained the state you were in. She said the last time she had seen you, you were sitting in a chair drinking a soda. She had no idea what could have happened to you."

Mom set a bowl of cereal on the table for each of us. I felt as if I was still in a daze. This couldn't be happening to me. I felt it all had to be a bad dream and that I would wake up from this crazy dream soon. I looked at Travis who was staring into his cereal bowl. "Travis, I'm so sorry I put you through this; you always know when things aren't quite right. I feel like such a fool."

Travis came over to me and put his arms around me hugging me tightly. "Ana, I just know how Satan works. He goes after new Christians and tries to discourage them. Has it worked yet? Are you discouraged?"

Not wanting to ever let go of Travis, I gently responded, "I think if it hadn't been for you Travis, I certainly would be discouraged. I thank God for you."

We continued talking as Travis finished his cereal, then we all went into the living room. Travis and I sat on the soft couch. Travis told us he had a story he wanted to share with us to help me understand why he worries about me so much. "I've never shared this story with you, but I think now would be a good time to tell you. It's kind of hard to talk about, but I hope it will make you understand why I was so worried about you at that party Ana." Travis looked a little uneasy, leaning forward with his elbows resting on his knees. "I had a brother who was two years older than me. His name was Daniel. He loved playing baseball and he was very good. Daniel played Little League and was on an All-Star Team. He was a strong Christian and a wonderful brother. One night, he too was invited to a party. One of his friends pressured him to try some drugs and Daniel ended up overdosing. His friend never forgave himself and committed suicide shortly after my brother died. Two lives were ruined just by going to a party and giving into peer pressure."

My heart was saddened by what Travis must have gone through when Daniel died. No wonder he was

Chapter 16

upset when I told him I was going to a party. I hugged Travis tighter than I had ever hugged him before.

He added, "I hope you're not mad at me for busting in on the party and taking you home."

I couldn't believe he thought I would be mad at him for helping me, so I told him emphatically, "No way am I mad at you for anything you did to help me! I don't even want to think what would have happened to me if you hadn't shown up when you did. I'll be forever in your debt.

"I agree with Ana, Travis! We will forever be indebted to you for saving Ana," Mom exclaimed.

I began to feel much better after getting coffee and food into my system. Travis stayed with me the rest of the day and later that afternoon we went to the church and talked to Pastor Dave. We shared with him all that had happened the night before. He thought very carefully about his reply, and after much thought he told me what he had said to his kids. "If you walk down a dark alley, expect dark things to happen, and be afraid, be very afraid. If you don't want to be afraid, then walk in the light of day. Jesus is the light; always stay close to Him by prayer and obedience."

He was glad everything had turned out as well as it did. After talking with Dave for awhile, Travis and I left his office and decided to go see "Titanic", just the two of us.

On our way to the movie, we both called our parents to make sure they were okay with us going to a movie. After getting their approval, we grabbed a bite to eat and then went to the movie. Neither of us had seen The Titanic yet and really wanted to see it. It was a long movie, but it succeeded in taking our minds off what could have been a disastrous day, at least for a little while. We really enjoyed the movie and I noticed a few tears rolling down Travis's cheeks along with me. After the movie we went to Shari's for a piece of pie, since we knew they stayed open late. I ordered my favorite pie, coconut cream while Travis had apple pie ala mode. We talked about the night before and how I felt I had betrayed God. Travis reminded me, a temptation isn't a sin until you follow through with the act. He also reminded me that I hadn't willingly taken the drug that was given to me. Nevertheless, I still felt bad. I should never have gone to the party; I only wanted to be with my friends and not disappoint them.

Chapter 16

Reaching across the table to take my hand, Travis reassured me that everybody makes mistakes, and that if we learn from them, it's sometimes worth the pain.

I gave him a look of disbelief. "It seems like you never make the mistakes that I do." He disagreed with me and explained they're just different kinds of mistakes. Travis took me home. He walked me to the door and I thought he might give me a kiss, but I was wrong. He gave me a hug and kissed the top of my head. Then walking to the car, he smiled, waved his hand and left. I never heard from Sara or Riley, but that didn't really surprise me. I was a little hurt that they didn't care enough about me to call and find out how I was doing. That night before dropping off to sleep, I asked God to watch over Sara and Riley and to help them somehow find Him and accept Him into their lives. Just before I drifted off to sleep, I whispered a special prayer. "Thank you, God for putting Travis in my life and for watching over me."

Chapter 17

There were only a few weeks until school started, and I still wanted to talk to the little girl at the park. I kept watching for her. It was a friday night and to my amazement I looked out the window and there she was, sitting in the sandbox. I ran down the stairs and out the door. When I reached the sandbox, I couldn't believe my eyes. Travis was sitting beside her. I stood there in shock.

When Travis realized I was there he looked up and said, "Oh Ana look who I found! This is Amanda. Amanda, this is my friend, Ana."

I sat down beside Travis. Amanda had red hair and dark brown eyes. She sifted the sand between her toes as she greeted me. Travis leaned close to Amanda and whispered to her. She looked up at me with those big eyes and giggled.

Chapter 17

I spoke up and said, "No fair, what did Travis say to you?"

Amanda looked at Travis, then with her hand made a motion as if she were zipping up her lips.

I responded with, "I see whose side you're on." We all laughed, and Travis said he needed to get home. He stood up, waved and left. I told Amanda about my sisters and that I had seen her at the airport once with an older lady.

"That's my grandma, Sue." She started to tell me when suddenly she stopped.

I asked her what she was doing in Portland with her grandma and she said that she was just visiting. I tried to tell her about my family, hoping she would be more open with me, but it didn't work. She wouldn't share any more. I asked her if she had lots of friends and she said she didn't. I didn't want to pry too much so I gave up on questioning her for now. I asked her if she wanted to go on the swings with me but again she said she didn't want to. I didn't know what else to say to her, so I just sat with her in silence. I heard someone call for her to come home, so we both got up and left. I went home feeling very disappointed I hadn't gotten any information from her. I watched the park whenever I was home to see if Amanda would show up there again. As soon as I saw her, I would run over to the park and spend time with her. I wouldn't ask too many questions, hoping to gain her trust. Maybe one day she would share with me. I prayed for Amanda every night when I said my prayers. I knew in my heart there was something she was afraid to talk about, but I didn't know what it could be. Travis met me at the park as well, but Amanda usually wouldn't come if he was there, which surprised him and me both, since he was the one who had made the initial contact with her. School was going to start in about three weeks and I was hoping Amanda would talk to me soon.

Chapter 18

Travis and I went to the Western Idaho State Fair, scheduled two weeks before school starts, so it doesn't interfere with the first day of school. We went on the rides, ate lots of food and walked through the tents showing all the different farm animals. After a long day at the fair and a lot of walking, we took a break and sat down on one of the benches close to the big water fountain in front of an exposition building. As we sat there holding hands, we talked and just enjoyed each other's company. Looking up and across the way I saw Amanda with a tall man. I told Travis to look up as I showed him where Amanda was walking with the man. I grabbed Travis's hand and pulled him to where Amanda and the man were standing. They had stopped in front of a concession stand to buy a corndog. We walked over to the concession stand and stood behind them and waited until Amanda turned and saw us. She pulled on the hand of the man and said, "Oh, hi."

"Hi, Amanda," we both responded simultaneously.

The man Amanda was with gave me a look I will never forget. It was as if he were saying, "Leave us alone."

Amanda turned to the man and said, "Dad, this is Ana, the girl at the park I was telling you about."

He replied, "And this must be Travis her friend. It's nice to meet you both."

His words didn't match the look on his face. He didn't seem happy to meet us at all. This must be Amanda's Dad, I thought to myself. Abruptly, Amanda and her Dad turned and disappeared into the crowd. We tried to see where they went but were unable to find them. We decided to stay a while longer and ride some more rides. It was dark, and the lights of the fair were beautiful at night. We rode the big Ferris wheel and we ended up sitting at the very top. It was a beautiful view from there. We could see the entire Boise valley all lit up in the warm summer night air. It was so peaceful just sitting on the top of the world with Travis.

Chapter 18

After awhile, Travis put his hand under my chin and leaned over and kissed me softly on the cheek. Then he whispered in my ear, "I love you."

I looked into his eyes and asked, "Did I just hear what I thought I heard?"

He nodded his head, confirming what I thought I had heard him say. I took his face in both of my hands and proudly said, "I love you too." I leaned over and kissed Travis on the cheek, before he could say a word.

The next day, I looked for Amanda most of the day in the park, but she never showed up. Travis came over for dinner that night and then we went to the park to see if Amanda would come. We talked about the day ahead hoping we would be in a few classes together. Tomorrow was the first day of the new school year. It was starting to get dark when we finally saw Amanda begin walking across the street. She must have seen Travis and me because suddenly she turned and started going back towards her house. I jumped to my feet and ran to catch up, with Travis right on my heels. I grabbed her, and she tried to pull away.

She cried out, "Let me go."

I asked her why she had turned to leave when she saw us in the park. She denied that she was leaving because of us. I knelt down, so I could look her in the eye and pleaded with her to tell me what was wrong, and she simply said, "I want to go home! Leave me alone!"

I held on to her and I said to her as plainly as I could. "Amanda, something is wrong. Why can't you tell us?"

She replied, "Because, I'll get in trouble."

I pleaded with her and told her that she could trust us and that we only wanted to help. She began crying and told us she was afraid. She pleaded with me to let her go. I felt that if I let her go we would never be able to help her. I didn't know what else to do, so I let her go.

As she ran home, Travis and I stood there together. Travis held me as I cried. I yelled out to God to help Amanda, since I couldn't. Travis went to my house with me and stayed awhile, talking and trying to comfort me. I knew I wasn't the one that needed comforting. I really felt that Amanda needed help and soon.

The next morning, I gathered everything I needed for the first day of school and waited for Travis to pick

Chapter 18

me up in his car. As we drove down the street, I couldn't help but notice as we rounded the corner, Amanda and an older lady getting into a taxi. I believe the woman was Amanda's grandmother. I couldn't believe what I was seeing and was in total shock! "Travis, look! What's going on? Amanda should be going to school! Where is she taking her?" We continued heading to school, but I had a hard time keeping my mind on my classes. All I could think about was getting home to see if I could find out anything about Amanda.

Travis stayed at my house until Mom and Jim came home from work.

"What's going on with you two?" She could tell that we had something on our minds. We told Jim and Mom what had happened with Amanda and us. How we had tried to get her to talk to us and how she told us she couldn't tell us. We explained to them what we had witnessed on our way to school. Mom sat down in her oversized chair sinking in with her feet stretched out on top of a foot stool.

"I may be able to help you two solve this mystery. I know someone who works with Amanda's dad," she said. "Ana, will you get me a phonebook and the phone? Mom looked up a phone number and dialed it. She talked to the person for some time and then hung up the phone.

"What did you find out, Mom?"

She paused and told us both to sit down.

"Mom, what is it?" I insisted.

She slowly began telling us what she had found out about Amanda and her situation. "Amanda's dad has been arrested for molesting Amanda. Amanda's mom is mentally ill and can't take care of Amanda, so Amanda's grandmother came to get Amanda, to take her to Portland with her. Amanda's mom was put in a mental hospital and they're hoping to get her back on her medication. She said Amanda's dad had kept her Mom from taking her medication, so she wouldn't know what he was doing to Amanda."

I couldn't believe what I was hearing! "How did they find out?" I asked Mom.

"I guess Amanda told her Grandmother last night and that's why she took her away this morning. The police came to his workplace and arrested her dad early this morning." Mom answered.

Chapter 18

We were all in a state of shock with what had just transpired. The days ahead were hard. I wanted to see Amanda in the worst way, but it just wasn't possible since she was with her grandmother in Portland. Amanda's dad pled guilty, so there wasn't a trial. I was happy Amanda wouldn't have to go through the horrible ordeal of testifying in court. Oh how, I wanted to see her so badly, but that wouldn't happen.

My life went on and I thought of Amanda, hoping her life was not ruined forever. Travis and I went through school together and then on to Boise State University. We graduated and married in 2004. It was a beautiful wedding and such a beautiful, bright, sunny day. Something amazing happened after the reception as we came out of the church and left for our honeymoon. The sky was blue over the church, but in the distance was a group of dark clouds. There was the most amazing rainbow stretching above us as we ran to our car. When everyone saw it, you could hear the "ahs" uttered through the small crowd of friends and family. It was as if God was putting his own stamp of approval on our marriage.

Chapter 19

A couple of years passed and one day the phone rang. I went to answer it and to my surprise it was a girl's voice. I said, "Hello."

She answered, "Hi Ana, this is Amanda."

I almost dropped the phone, I was so stunned! I composed myself and then replied, "Hi Amanda." I asked her how she had found me, and she said she had found Travis's mom who led her to me. We talked for over an hour. She filled in all the questions I had after she left Boise and went to Portland all those years ago. She explained that she had called her grandmother that night she had talked to Travis and me in the park and told her everything her Dad had been doing to her. She thanked me for giving her the courage to get help. I told her I really didn't do anything, but she informed me that my concern for her is what gave her the courage to tell someone. She always felt nobody really cared

Chapter 19

for her except her grandmother. She didn't think her grandmother would be able to help her as much as she had. Her Dad always made her think she would never see her Mom again if she told anyone. She explained that her mother was able to get her medication regulated and is doing much better. "She has a job and we both live with my grandmother," she said.

It was so nice to hear from Amanda, I could hardly wait to tell Travis about the unexpected phone call. Amanda also asked if I remembered the time I had told her about my trip to the Oregon coast and the Bed and Breakfast I had stayed in and the lady who ran it, her name was Gloria. I vaguely remembered telling her about that summer, but not totally. Then she went on to explain about the same Bed and Breakfast I had stayed in. Her mom, grandmother and her, went for a few days and stayed there too. She said Gloria took them to the Camp for a church service and they all accepted Jesus as their Savior. Pure joy came over me as she told me about them all knowing Jesus. She thanked me again for all I had done for her and I was speechless. I invited Amanda to come and stay with us if she ever came to Boise and she said she would love to see me again.

CHAPTER 20

The next few years were busy with the new arrival of our beautiful baby girl Amanda, named after our little friend Amanda we met at the park. Travis is a big helper at church, doing the sound and sometimes being worship leader. I'm suspicious that Pastor Dave is working toward trying to convince Travis to become a pastor, and I'm sure Travis hasn't realized it quite yet. Travis would be a wonderful pastor.

It was almost time for Travis to arrive home and I was getting dinner ready. Amanda was busy on the floor playing with her toys; she was good at occupying herself. I heard Travis as he drove into the garage and Amanda did as well. Travis opened the door and Amanda crawled as fast as her little legs would carry her, into the arms of her daddy. Travis's face beamed as he came walking into the kitchen to greet me with a big kiss.

"How was your day, babe?" Travis muttered as he grabbed the mail with his empty hand, holding Amanda close to his chest with the other.

I answered back with a grin, "I had a wonderful day."

He looked up from the mail he was sorting, tossing the junk mail in a throw away pile. He wasn't sure whether to believe me or not. He put Amanda down on the floor and walked behind me and gave me a big hug and whispered in my ear, "I sure love you." He nibbled my ear and turned to go into the living room for his nightly ritual. First, he finished sorting the mail, took off his shoes, putting them away in the bedroom; then he changed out of his suit and tie into something more comfortable.

I could hear him walk down the hall towards the kitchen saying, "Boy that sure smells good. Is it what I think it is?"

I smiled and answered, "Yes, it's your favorite, meatloaf." Travis could eat almost the whole pan of meatloaf, but we usually save some leftovers for the next day's lunch for a sandwich. Travis is always good about helping me with the dishes, so we can both have time to spend with Amanda before she goes to bed.

Chapter 20

It's always my favorite time of the day, watching him with her. It fills my heart with such amazing love for Travis. I often wonder if God ever looks down at us and thinks the same about us, "Oh, look at Ana, isn't she the sweetest woman?"

Every night we give Amanda a bath, get her in her pajamas, and read her a story. We pray with her, lay her down in her crib and she falls off to sleep. Travis and I usually turn on some Christian music and sit on the couch and talk about things that might be on our minds. "Oh, by the way, I forgot to tell you that Pastor Dave asked if I would go to the jail and visit a man that used to go to our church. There are set visiting hours at the jail, and he has a wedding during those times. Is it okay if I go fill in for Pastor Dave?" Travis asked.

I thought about it for a moment and then said, "Yes, sure, I have no problem with it, go ahead."

Travis wouldn't be going to the jail for a couple of days. We prayed together, asking for guidance to say the right words and to keep him from being nervous. He had never done jail ministry before. I knew there wouldn't be any problems for him. The day for the visit to the jail finally arrived; he was going directly after work. He had taken some clothes with him, so he could change before he went to the jail.

It was just after lunch when the phone rang. It was Travis. "Hi babe, what are you doing?" He usually didn't call me during the day because of his busy schedule at the bank. He worked his way up to vice-president, which meant I could stay home with Amanda.

I nervously responded, "I just put Amanda down for a nap and was getting ready to clean up the lunch dishes. Is everything ok?"

I could tell there was something wrong by the sound of his voice. "I hate asking you to do this Ana, but I have no choice. Would you be able to go to the jail for me?"

"Oh, Travis, I really don't think I could do that. I wouldn't know what to say or do."

"Let me explain, Ana. I just found out about a meeting that I need to attend, and I can't get out of it. Believe me, I've already tried. Please Ana."

I hate it when he pleads with me. I can never say no to him when he says please. I finally gave in. "Okay Travis, but you owe me big time."

Chapter 20

I could hear a sigh of relief in his voice as he began thanking me over, and over again. "Thank you, thank you, and thank you. I married the best woman ever."

"Okay, okay, that's enough. I'm not sure how much good I'll do. I'm not nearly as natural as you are, but I will give it my best effort."

I said goodbye to Travis, then called my mother-in-law to see if she could babysit for me while I went to the jail. She was always willing to take care of Amanda whenever I needed someone. Amanda was the first grandchild to both my mom and my mother-in-law. I was almost wishing she would tell me she couldn't watch her, but I wasn't that lucky. She said, "I would love to see my little grandbaby girl."

I dressed Amanda in a cute little red dress with black shoes. I brushed her hair and put a ponytail on top of her head. I buckled Amanda in her car seat, drove over to my mother in-laws house, dropped off Amanda and proceeded to the jail. I prayed as I drove, "Please Jesus, help me. I'm not sure I can do this. I'll need you to direct my words and guide me."

I had never been to the jail before, so I wasn't sure what to do. I followed the signs and was soon in a room where there were several people. I noticed a woman inside a caged window. I waited my turn and after awhile, she motioned for me to go to a table. Directly behind me was a form for me to fill out my personal information and information about the person I was intending on visiting. Travis had luckily remembered to call me back and give me what I needed on the phone right before Amanda woke up from her nap. I took the form back up to the counter, but she told me to hang on to it until 6:30 p.m. She explained, "At that time, get in line and when it's your turn I will stamp your hand and then you will be guaranteed your visit. We only let in 30 people at a time. You don't have to stay and wait. You can leave and then come back at 7:00 p.m." She seemed very nice and friendly. I decided to stay because people were already making a line by the window and I wanted to make sure I made it within the 30 people.

There were already six people in front of me and I was lucky enough to be where there was a bench with enough room for about four people. Next to me was a woman who didn't seem to know the routine either. She smiled at me and I smiled back. She began telling

Chapter 20

me she was here to see her son. I felt sorry for her as she spoke. I couldn't imagine having to visit any of my children in a place such as this. She had wonderful brown eyes and blonde hair. She was a large woman, but it didn't seem to matter. Her smile was warm with love. She asked me who I was here for and I began to tell her about Travis and how he was the one that originally was going to visit. She seemed interested and the look of compassion upon her face enveloped her, which made it easy to share with her. I explained who I was visiting and how I was only helping Travis out. She also seemed interested about the work of our pastor and she said she was hoping her pastor was going to visit her son as well. "So what church do you go to?" she asked.

"We go to a church called The Living Word."

"Oh, I've heard of that church. I used to know someone who attended it."

"What were their names?" I asked.

"I don't remember their names. It was too long ago."

I apologized and asked her about her church. She paused for a moment and slowly told me about her church. You could tell she had a great passion for it and the people there. It wasn't a big church, but it did many great things for God. "If you can believe it, I'm in the church praise band."

It was nice to be able to talk to someone who was a fellow Christian. Just then I noticed the line moving toward the lady at the window. We stood up and then it was my turn to put my hand through the slit in the window. The lady stamped my hand with blue ink that read "Ada County Jail". I decided to stay, but the lady I was talking with had left with the same stamp on her hand.

I sat on the bench and waited until it was time to go in. It was interesting watching the different people waiting with me. I was wishing the time would pass quickly and it did. Soon it was time; it was 6:45 p.m. and people started lining up again.

We all had to go through a metal detector, which took some time. We were then guided into a long hallway, with a door at the end. We all managed to squish inside, and I noticed that the lady I had been talking with was at the very back. Once we made it in, the door opened in front of us and we proceeded to another hallway. After arriving in the next hallway, the

Chapter 20

door closed behind us, with a loud clanging sound. It was eerie, hearing the door locking behind us... There was no going back. The door opened in front of us and we all started filing down a long hallway.

We finally reached a room that had phones and stools in individual stalls. A glass window separated us from the person we were visiting. It made me feel better to see there wasn't physical contact with them. I sat down and soon a man was led to my stall. He sat down in front of me and we both picked up the phone. I introduced myself and Jeff said, "Thanks for coming to see me." It seemed I did most of the talking until I told him I was married to Travis. It was like I had lit a fire under his stool. I didn't realize he had grown up with Travis and had gone to his church with him before I started going there. "I wish I hadn't left the church. Maybe I wouldn't be here in this hell hole." Jeff announced.

I encouraged him to come back to church when he gets out and told him it was never too late to change. He nodded and thanked me for coming to visit with him. He explained that his family had given up on him. After all, he had put them all through so much, and he didn't blame them. The guard announced it was time to leave. I asked if he would like me to pray with him and he nodded his head and I prayed with him.

I knew that's exactly what Travis would have done. I said goodbye to Jeff and said, "I'll see you in church." I turned and walked back down to the end of the hall and went through the same process we all did earlier, only in reverse. We all filed back into the main room where we had started from. I was in the front of the line again and was hoping to see the lady I had been talking to earlier. Finally, I spotted her. She was one of the last to come out. She noticed me waiting and smiled as she neared me.

"How did it go?" she asked

"It went fine." I responded. "How did it go with your son?"

She shrugged her shoulders and I saw a tear well up in her eyes. I reached to give her a hug, but she pulled back. She gently took me by the shoulders and firmly stated, "I will never give up on Josh and more importantly neither will God."

Suddenly something she said triggered a conversation I had with a lady about God many years ago. I

Chapter 20

nodded in agreement with what she had just said. Then I asked, "Can I ask what your name is?"

She had a strange look on her face as she said her name, "Wanda."

I couldn't believe my ears. I replied to her, "Wanda, I'm Ana."

Wanda stared at me in disbelief. I heard her saying over, and over again, "No way! No way! Do you know how much I've thought about you over the years? I prayed that one day I would get to see you again, and here you are."

She wrapped her arms around me and held me close. We were both crying. Neither of us seemed to worry about what we looked like, because both of our prayers had been answered.

THE END

About the Author

Wanda Terry is a faith-based Christian, who has lived in Boise, Idaho for more than 60 years. She has two grown sons and many grandchildren. She has worked as a Hairdresser for 40 years. Her experience with prison ministry as a young woman has inspired her love of the broken and her drive for the unsaved. Her faith in Christ Jesus has taken her through her own challenges in life.

CPSIA information can be obtained
at www.ICGtesting.com
Printed in the USA
FFHW020156021118
49223213-53431FF